Silent Life and Silent Language

GALLAUDET CLASSICS IN DEAF STUDIES

A SERIES EDITED BY
Kristen C. Harmon

Silent Life and Silent Language

The Inner Life of a Mute in an Institution for the Deaf

Kate M. Farlow

Introduction by
Kristen C. Harmon

GALLAUDET UNIVERSITY PRESS
Washington, DC

Gallaudet University Press
Washington, DC 20002
http://gupress.gallaudet.edu

Library of Congress Cataloging-in-Publication Data

Names: Farlow, Kate M., author. | Harmon, Kristen, writer of introduction.
Title: Silent life and silent language : the inner life of a mute in an
    institution for the deaf / Kate M. Farlow ; introduction by Kristen C.
    Harmon.
Other titles: Inner life of a mute in an institution for the deaf Description:
    Washington, D.C. : Gallaudet University Press, 2018. | Series: Gallaudet
    classics deaf studies ; 11 | A reissue of the edition published in 1883.
Identifiers: LCCN 2018013364| ISBN 9781944838294 (paperback) | ISBN
    9781944838300 (e-book)
Subjects: LCSH: Deaf children—Education—United States—19th
    century—Fiction. | Deaf children—19th century—Fiction. | Mute
    persons—19th century—Fiction. | Indiana Asylum for the Education
    of the Deaf and Dumb—Fiction. | BISAC: SOCIAL SCIENCE /
    People with Disabilities. | FICTION / Biographical. | GSAFD:
    Autobiographical fiction.
Classification: LCC PS3606.A712 S55 2018 | DDC 813/.6—dc23
LC record available at https://lccn.loc.gov/2018013364

∞ This paper meets the requirements of ANSI/NISO Z39.48-1992
(Permanence of Paper).

In "dumb signifants" we speak,
And many happy hours spend
With thoughts that other hands have penned.
In voiceless song to God we raise
A psalm of grateful love and praise.

Contents

Author's Preface

My design in writing this book was to give the public a fair idea of life in an institution for the deaf and dumb; and to show what has been done, and can still be done, for those deprived of the senses of hearing and speech. I also wish to disabuse the minds of parents who think their deaf-mute children will not be well cared for and receive benefit in these institutions. I can say from my own experience they certainly are a blessing to the deaf and dumb; for I am myself a deaf-mute and have been educated in one of these institutions.

It is through my life there that I have obtained the material for my story. Most of the colloquies that occur, and a few of the incidents, were merely composed to bring out some important truths concerning the deaf and dumb; but the story itself is founded on facts. The names given to the characters are not the real names of the persons, but most anyone who dwelt in the institution with the writer will, I think, be able to assign to most of the characters represented their proper names.

There is much still to be said on my subject which "the state of my purse" will not permit me to say in this volume. It is my intention, should this meet with success, to write another book on the subject, detailing my life as a teacher in another institution for the deaf and dumb where new methods of teaching, new arrangements, etc., were observed.

This book will, I trust, interest all who read it, and may give to many new ideas concerning this once unfortunate class of human beings.

Crude though the work may be, yet I hope it will be kindly received. With a silent prayer that it may be the means of doing good, I send it out into the wide world.

K. M. F.

Introduction

Kristen C. Harmon

Silent Life and Silent Language: The Inner Life of a Mute in an Institution for the Deaf is a record of life at a Midwestern residential school between 1869 and 1875. Like the author, Kate M. Farlow (1854–1909), the protagonist of this embellished memoir was deafened in childhood from meningitis and entered what Farlow calls in this book the "I_____ Institution" (the Indiana School for the Deaf). As Farlow notes in her preface, "It is through my life [at the Indiana School for the Deaf] that I have obtained the material for my story. Most of the colloquies that occur, and a few of the incidents, were merely composed to bring out some important truths concerning the deaf and dumb; but the story itself is founded on facts" (ix).*

There are few accounts written by American Deaf women in the nineteenth century, and this episodic memoir is all the more remarkable in that it gives a detailed accounting of daily life and learning in a deaf school from someone who experienced it. The forty-two short chapters with descriptive titles such as "Some Glimpses into the Condition and Doings of Deaf-Mutes" and "Some Birthday Customs" include nostalgic and thorough descriptions of the local foods that were served on a daily basis, sumptuous holiday feasts, daily and seasonal play activities, and the training that young Deaf men and women of that era received in the residential schools.

Farlow wrote *Silent Life and Silent Language* with the intention of helping hearing parents of deaf children understand that their

---

* Numbers in parentheses refer to pages in this volume.

child's deafness was not a door closing; rather, with the right access and right community, they would be "enabled to be blessings and helps . . . instead of being objects to be looked down upon by their hearing brothers and sisters" (180). She states in the preface that her "design in writing this book was to give the public a fair idea of life in an institution for the deaf and dumb; and to show what has been done, and can still be done, for those deprived of the senses of hearing and speech. I also wish to disabuse the minds of parents who think their deaf-mute children will not be well cared for and receive benefit in these institutions" (ix).

In many ways, this fictionalized memoir presages the accounts of Deaf lives written for hearing parents of deaf children by some 100 years. Farlow was an early advocate of residential schools, along with what was then called "the sign method" and Deaf community life and letters, and her support is evident in her depiction of the signing deaf children and teens in this work. She gives advice that will feel quite familiar to contemporary readers. For example, she is aware of the impact of what we now call language deprivation and the sensitive period of language acquisition.

In addition to advocating for accessible education through the description of daily life at a thriving residential school, Farlow provides detailed descriptions of mid-to-late nineteenth-century American Sign Language and gestures that will prove of interest to sign language linguists, anthropologists, educators, and historians. Farlow's descriptions of buildings, landscapes, and rooms also provide a great deal of period detail for historians and architects. There are even some hints of ideas that foreshadow "Deaf Space" by some 125+ years. Descriptions of Deaf games and ASL story nights are also included, and Deaf Studies scholars and students will likely find the description of white Deaf residential school life and gender-segregated activities and spaces to be revealing.

*

After graduating in 1875 from the Indiana Asylum for the Education of the Deaf and Dumb—as it was then called—Farlow went on to become a teacher at the Iowa School for the Deaf in 1880. She spent at least three years there and then left Iowa for Cheney, Kansas, where she was active in the Deaf community. Around 1896, Farlow relocated to Ohio to live with her parents on a farm.[1] In 1899, *The Silent Worker* noted that Farlow had written a manuscript called *Prisoner of Silence* and that she needed a specific number of "subscriptions" to underwrite the publication of this piece. This manuscript has not been located, nor does it seem to have been published. The Farlow family moved to Michigan, where Farlow became a caretaker for the girls at the Michigan School for the Deaf in 1902.[2] By this time, she had become a regular correspondent to the Little Paper Family's *Ohio Chronicle*, the newspaper published by the Ohio School for the Deaf.

Farlow wrote poetry and short, newsy, pieces in *The Ohio Chronicle* about personal, family, and community life.[3] Over the years, she described increasing difficulties with her health, her eyesight, and work. At one point in 1907, after suffering what she calls "dropsical heart disease" and near-blindness, she went to Philadelphia to sell hosiery door-to-door.[4] Around this time, Farlow wrote and attempted to publish another book, *In Still Ways*; however, she was defrauded by the company that bought the rights to this book. She paid out a sum of $50 (possibly to buy back the rights), which she never recovered, but she resolutely noted in her "Michigan Letter" in 1907 that she paid off the debt by selling "stereoscopic views." As far as can be determined, *In Still Ways* never was published.[5]

✳

Farlow was a devout Christian and this sensibility pervades much of her published work and her choice of publisher—Christian Publishing House in Dayton, Ohio. Readers interested in religion in the Deaf community and in the teaching of religious history at deaf schools will find much in her memoir that provides insight into how Christian practices infused the curriculum and everyday life in nineteenth-century Midwestern Deaf schools like this one. Farlow's faith is evident in a poem she wrote in 1904 in *The Ohio Chronicle* as an homage to Gallaudet.

THE DEAF—PAST, PRESENT, AND FUTURE

Down the dim aisles of the past
We turn our gaze to-day;
But shapes of gloom like shadows cast
Obscure that far-off way....
But, lo! A ray of light illumes...
Forward into the future we gaze
With souls by high ambitions fired;
Be this our song through coming days,
Praise God, who hath all good inspired.
. . . .[6]

Farlow continued to publish her observations of quotidian life in her "Michigan Letters," a regular column in *The Ohio Chronicle*. Her notes on Midwestern weather, farming life, responses to letters reprinted in the paper, and the small dramas of family and community events have a casual, epistolary style that contrasts with the dramatic rhetoric of her poetry and, occasionally, her narrative in *Silent Life and Silent Language*.

Nineteenth-century technology, transportation, and events play minor yet memorable roles in this manuscript. Chapter 20, "The Magic Lantern Entertainment," recounts a Saturday night magic lantern exhibition at the school. This chapter has been reprinted in a blog on the history of public entertainment and photography.[7] In chapter 26, Farlow tells the story of the accidental deaths of two residential school boys who did not hear an oncoming train. In keeping with historical accounts of life in the aftermath of the Civil War, this book contains descriptions of the somewhat sentimentalized military play-acting performed by the boys of the school, as well as military metaphors to describe sudden summer storms (see pp. 74, 75, 108).

Despite being set in Indiana in the years after the Civil War, there is little to no mention of the larger political and historical environment. Farlow was born in 1854, so she presumably had some idea of such large-scale national events. Because this book is a nostalgic memoir, it is possible that this lack of explicit connection to the larger society is a function of genre and the author's purpose. Further work on Farlow's literary context and influences and biography may shed some light on this question.

As an aspiring author of additional manuscripts, Kate Farlow seems to have found—like her heroine, Carrie Raymond—that "the romantic dream of her school days proved to be but a castle in the air, which, by and by, tumbled down; but strange to say, she did not mourn over its fall" (184). Even though Farlow was deeply affected by being defrauded by the publisher of her second book, and spoke of this disappointment until her death in 1909, she, like Carrie Raymond, seems to have carried on with resolute and "hearty" determination (39).

Kate Farlow died after an "illness of a few weeks" on April 18, 1909, at the age of 54, near Lamb, Michigan.[8] Her last piece in *The Ohio Chronicle*, published less than one month before she died, was a fond and humorous poem, "The Neighborhood Baby," and it ends with a figurative wink to the reader over a toddler's sudden discovery that a new baby "sisser" has dethroned him from his status as the cherished neighborhood baby. In a cameo appearance, Farlow seems to include herself in this poem.

> There Kate he finds to whom they speak
> In voiceless way when an answer they seek;
> So he wiggles his fingers at her too,
> What does he say—who knows? Do you?[9]

A determined observer of seemingly "silenced" experiences and overlooked lives and languages, Farlow provides a fascinating and revealing glimpse into mid-to-late nineteenth-century deaf school life and learning.

Notes

1. "City News," *Evening News* (Indianapolis, IN), June 29, 1875, 2; "Institution Items," *American Annals of the Deaf* 25, no. 4 (1880): 290; "Among the Alumni," *Ohio Chronicle*, May 22, 1909, 2; "Sun-flower State News," *Deaf Mute's Journal*, October 15, 1891, 4; "Ex-Pupils' Column," *Ohio Chronicle*, March 7, 1896, 2; "Home News," *Ohio Chronicle*, March 19, 1898, 3.

2. "Prisoner of Silence," *Silent Worker*, September 1899, 8; "Among Sister Schools," *Ohio Chronicle*, October 9, 1902, 2.

3. See, for example, Kate Farlow, "Deaf, Dumb, and Blind," *Ohio Chronicle*, February 23, 1901, 1; "Washington (Tune, America)," *Ohio Chronicle*, February 16, 1901, 1.

4. Kate Farlow, "From Kate Farlow," *Ohio Chronicle*, June 1, 1907, 1.

5. Kate Farlow, "Michigan Letter," *Ohio Chronicle*, October 9, 1907, 1.

6. "The Deaf—Past, Present, and Future," *Ohio Chronicle*, October 1, 1904, 1.

7. Luke McKernan, "Silent Life and Silent Language," *Picturegoing: Eyewitness Accounts of Viewing Pictures*, (blog), April 12, 2015, http://picturegoing.com/?p=4026.

8. "Obituaries," *Herald of Gospel Liberty* (Dayton, OH), May 13, 1909, 606.

9. "The Neighborhood Baby," *Ohio Chronicle*, March 27, 1909, 1.

Silent Life and Silent Language

1

An Illness, and Its Result

It was a beautiful spring morning. The sunlight fell in golden splendor down upon the green earth, making the dew drops glisten and sparkle like costly diamonds. A soft and soothing spring breeze was blowing, gently stirring the delicate green leaves that covered the trees in front of Dr. Gage's small white cottage. The bosoms of the little birds that now and then alighted upon these trees seemed filled to overflowing with gladness, so joyously did they sing.

Such was the outdoor scene presented to the eye and ear of Dr. Gage as he sat in his small but neat office from whence, through open door and window, he could catch glimpses of the outside world. He was trying to concentrate his thoughts upon a new and important medicinal treatise; but sickness, sorrow, pain, and death seemed so out of harmony with the life, and light, and beauty without that he found it impossible to become interested in his book and fell into a fit of musing.

Suddenly his train of thought was cut short by the appearance of a messenger at his open door, who said, "Doctor, you are wanted at Mr. Raymond's. Carrie Raymond is very sick."

At this announcement the doctor rose hastily to his feet, and, saying, "I will go in a few minutes," began his preparations.

Upon reaching Mr. Raymond's, he found Carrie moaning and tossing with pain. After feeling her pulse he turned to Mrs. Raymond and asked, "What were the first symptoms of illness which you observed?"

She replied, "I went into the parlor this morning and found her there, seated on the floor, with both hands clasped on the back of her neck, and crying bitterly. I asked her what was the matter, and she said her neck hurt. She also complained of pain in the head. I took her to bed at once and sent for you," continued Mrs. Raymond.

"It is well you acted promptly," replied the doctor. "I fear it is a case of *cerebro-spinal meningitis*, a very dangerous disease. I will call again in the morning, when I hope to be able to decide for a certainty the nature of the disease." Then giving Carrie a soothing medicine to ease the pain, he left.*

As Dr. Gage had thought, it proved to be a case of *cerebro-spinal meningitis*, and, in spite of care and the precautions taken, Carrie rapidly grew worse. For weeks she tossed to and fro, refusing food, meanwhile growing more and more feeble, till it seemed to the anxious watchers that speedy death was inevitable. But still, life lingered in the feeble frame, and at the end of two months a change came, and the doctor pronounced her out of danger. He was observed, however, to critically examine the pupil of her right eye, which looked inflamed and had a thin, whitish scum over it. "Is there anything serious the matter with that eye, doctor?" asked Mrs. Raymond, anxiously. The doctor did not reply at first, but when the question was repeated he answered, "I fear the sight is destroyed." Then, seeing the look of deep pain on her face, he added, "It is quite common for the disease to affect the eyesight, but it is not always permanent; and her left eye is all right."

From this time on, Carrie improved constantly. Her appetite, which had been entirely lacking for several weeks, now became ravenous. She would eat all it was thought prudent for her to

---

*Note to readers: Some punctuation and sentences have been modernized for clarity. However, phrases that were common at the time Farlow wrote (for example, *deaf-mute* and *deaf and dumb*) have been retained.

have and cry for more. As she became more convalescent an unaccountable change was noticed in her manner. She did not appear to understand anything that was said to her, and all sounds, even the songs of the birds, which she had always delighted to listen to, were unheeded. Then, too, her conduct was at times so strange that her parents and friends were puzzled and could not account for it. Dr. Gage could not or would not advance any theory in relation to these peculiarities in her manner and conduct. As time went on these strange symptoms increased and grew more incomprehensible. Sometimes, without any visible cause, Carrie would burst into a fit of weeping, and all efforts to comfort her would for a time prove futile. At other times she would complain that someone was mocking her, and nothing could convince her that she was mistaken. She grew so timid that she could not bear to be left in a dark room, even though she knew she was not alone. As soon as the light was extinguished, strange, weird shapes seemed to fill the room, and she would shriek and cry with terror until the lamp was relighted. So all night long a lamp was kept burning in her chamber. Her parents wondered what could be the matter, as she was not naturally a timid child.

While they thus wondered, a solution of the mystery came in a very unexpected way. One day two ladies were visiting at Mrs. Raymond's when one of them noticed Carrie's strange behavior and thoughtlessly said to her companion, "Do you think Carrie has lost her reason?" The lady thus addressed gave her inquirer a quick, reproachful look, as much as to say, "Hush"; but Mrs. Raymond, who was in the room at the time, heard the question and saw the look which answered it, and a great pain filled her heart. Could it be, thought she, that Carrie, her bright, joyous Carrie, the pride of her heart, was doomed to go through life bereft of reason? The thought, with all its dreadful import, was almost more than she could bear. There now seemed no question of doubt as to the fact that Carrie's mind was deranged. Suitable tests also proved, to their surprise and grief, that her sense of hearing was entirely gone!

These were dark days for Mr. and Mrs. Raymond. It seemed well-nigh impossible for them to discover any but gloomy aspects to the case, or even to find comfort in Cowper's beautiful lines.

Judge not the Lord by feeble sense,
But trust him for his grace:
Behind a frowning providence
He hides a smiling face.

But God, whom they served, had not left them in this trying ordeal. He was still constantly watching tenderly over them and theirs.

Carrie's strength came back so slowly that months went by before she was again able to walk. As soon as she had far enough recovered to make it advisable, her father took her to a "water cure," hoping she might be benefited by the mineral waters, and also hoping to meet with a physician who made diseases of the eye and ear a specialty. But he did not meet such a doctor, and Carrie had grown so fearful of strangers that he found it impossible to induce her to remain long among them. They soon returned home again.

Carrie's physical health now improved rapidly, and her parents also saw, with joy, that her mental derangement was slowly disappearing. She was, however, very quiet, never answering any questions put to her. This was conclusive proof that she was indeed deaf. Human companionship now seemed distasteful to her. In summer she would often wander away alone into the woods and fields to play, talking, as she went, to the trees and flowers, or to some imaginary but invisible persons. These wanderings sometimes extended to such a length of time that, her parents growing uneasy, one of them would start out in search of the little wanderer, usually meeting her trudging along homeward with her apron gathered up to form a basket in which she would be carrying mosses, shells, bright-colored pebbles, acorns, nuts, etc., or else with her hands full of ripe berries or beautiful flowers.

Mr. and Mrs. Raymond grieved sorely over Carrie's loss of hearing and made frequent efforts to secure medical aid whereby she might regain her power to hear, but without avail. Carrie herself was but faintly conscious of her loss. It dawned upon her mind only gradually as her reason returned. A friend, in commenting upon this fact, said, "I believe that God has some wise design in thus afflicting her, and that this darkening of the mind was sent temporarily to break the force of the grief and mental pain which a too sudden awakening to a full consciousness of her altered condition might naturally produce. Yes," continued the friend, "I feel convinced that good and not evil will result from this seemingly unmitigated misfortune."

God works in a mysterious way,
His wonders to perform.

"And 'his ways are not our ways, nor his thoughts our thoughts.'"

Three years from the time Carrie became ill we find her fully restored, both bodily and mentally. She being now twelve years old, Mr. Raymond is advised to send her to the state institution for the deaf and dumb, to be educated.

2

Mr. Raymond Visits the Institution for the Deaf and Dumb

When the subject of sending Carrie to an institution for the deaf and dumb was first broached, both Mr. and Mrs. Raymond felt decidedly averse to the proposal. They did not like the idea of parting with her on any account. But they were very anxious to have her well educated, feeling that not only her earthly happiness and welfare, but her eternal interests, in a great degree, depended upon this. It was feared, however, that possibly the expense would be beyond their means. After some time spent in thought concerning the matter, Mr. Raymond decided to visit the institution of his state, located at I——, to learn the terms upon which pupils were admitted, and, if possible, secure for Carrie all the advantages the institution afforded. Accordingly, one pleasant August day he took the train bound for the city, and before many hours had gone by found himself at the institution. He was ushered by a servant into the presence of a small-sized, pleasant-looking gentleman, whose black hair and beard, thickly streaked with gray, suggested the fact that he had reached life's meridian, and was journeying towards the setting sun. To this gentleman, who proved to be the superintendent of the institution, Mr. Raymond told the story of Carrie's illness and how it had resulted in the loss of her hearing. Having finished the narrative, he said, "Now, if I can be assured that she will be well and properly cared for, and the charges are not beyond my ability to pay, I wish to have her placed under instruction here." When he had finished, the superintendent said,

"I can guarantee that she will be kindly treated, and tenderly and carefully cared for; and as to the costs of education, board, etc., these are all defrayed by the state." Taking a report of the institution from his desk, he read the following:

The institution is open to all the deaf and dumb children in the state, of suitable age and capacity for receiving instruction, and is free of charge for boarding and lodging, instruction, schoolbooks, and medical attendance, on conformity to the rules. The age for admission should be from nine to twenty-one years. None below nine nor over twenty-one can be admitted, except by a special act of the Board of Trustees. The institution is a school of learning, and not an asylum; and no one will be admitted or retained as a pupil who, from sickness, or from any other cause, is unable to pursue successfully the prescribed course of study. And if any pupil, after a fair trial, shall prove incorrigible or incompetent for useful instruction, such pupil shall thereupon be removed. Applicants from other states may be admitted as pupils by agreeing to pay two hundred dollars each, per session of forty weeks, payable quarterly in advance, provided they can be accommodated without excluding any deaf-mutes eligible to receive instruction, and who are citizens of the state.

"The enforcement of these rules is very essential," said the superintendent, laying down the book. "Without them," he continued, "the institution would be the prey of lawless and ineligible characters, or else so overcrowded with deaf-mutes too young, or too old, or otherwise incapacitated for receiving an education, that neither health nor comfort could be guaranteed to any of its inmates. The number of deaf-mutes of suitable age for receiving an education in the state is large, and this number seems constantly increasing; therefore, the state can allow to each pupil but a limited period of time in which to secure an education at the public expense. Seven terms of nine months each, with a single vacation each year, extending from the middle of June to the middle of September, is the time now granted to each pupil. Your daughter will be allowed that length of time to finish her education, which time, considering the advancement you say she has already made, will, I think, be quite sufficient for her to secure all the advantages necessary to success in life. She should, if possible, be brought to the institution promptly at the opening of every term, so as to secure all the advantages it is in our power to bestow."

Mr. Raymond promised to have Carrie promptly at school at the beginning of the next term, should no unforeseen event prevent, and arose to take his leave, expressing himself as thoroughly pleased with all he had seen of the institution.

When Mr. Raymond, by means of writing in print, told Carrie of their intention to send her to a school for the deaf and dumb, where she would be taught a great many things, her first question was, "Will they teach me to sing?" Mr. Raymond smiled when this question was asked, but answered, "Perhaps they will." Carrie had, when quite young, learned to sing simple songs by hearing her mother and others sing them, and had acquired a deep love for song; therefore, this question was quite a natural one.

The time for the opening of the next term of school was fast approaching, and preparations for Carrie's departure were pushed forward rapidly.

3

Carrie's Life in the Institution Commences

The fresh green of the summer foliage was fast changing to hues of crimson and gold; ripe, luscious fruit hung temptingly from the limbs of the orchard trees, and summer's heat had given place to the cool, fresh breezes of early autumn when Carrie left her home, and, in company with her father, mother, and little sister Minnie, departed on the train for the institution for the deaf and dumb, where the greater part of her time for seven years or more was to be spent. A pleasant ride of a few hours brought them to the city. Entering an omnibus, they were driven through the populous streets of the city towards its eastern suburb. Here they entered what seemed to be a park, with beautifully smooth lawns, still green, and dotted here and there with clumps and groups of tall evergreens and grand old forest trees. Up the smooth drive, winding between rows of trees, the omnibus passed swiftly and soon halted in front of a long building, towering story above story, high into the air, presenting so commodious yet neat an aspect. Mounting a long flight of white granite steps, they paused for a moment upon the broad portico, the massive pillars of which, rising upward for two stories, inspired Carrie with a sense of awe. Presently Carrie's father rang the doorbell, and they were soon shown into the reception room and received a warm welcome from Mr. M——, the superintendent, whose kind expression of countenance and warm greeting at once won Carrie's goodwill.

After arrangements had been perfected whereby Carrie was admitted to the institution and all its advantages, her parents spent a brief time in inspecting some of the rooms of the vast building, and then they were obliged to take leave of her and hurry away to the next train for home.

Carrie was then conducted into a large room and placed in the charge of two pretty little girls of about her own age. For a few hours she was much pleased with her newfound friends. She watched with amused interest their swift, though by her uncomprehended, motions, as they conversed together. She went with them from room to room, inspecting with childish curiosity the various arrangements, and tried, in her feeble, untrained way, to talk to them.

By and by the dinner hour came, and Carrie was placed between two of a row of girls, and soon they all marched down to the dining room. She did not enjoy the dinner. It was all so different to what she had been accustomed to at home; and so she felt shy and ill at ease. She was laughed at for the awkward manner in which she passed the pitcher of water from the girl on her right to the one on her left, and rebuked for holding her piece of pie in her hand instead of placing it on her plate, cutting it with her knife, and then conveying the pieces to her mouth with her fork. By this time she felt that she was losing what little self-possession and self-control she had, and arose to leave the table. But this was against the rules; so she was promptly motioned back to her seat.

After the meal was over she went into the large study room, where, laying her head down upon one of the many desks, she covered her face with her hands and burst into tears. The storm of her grief soon spent itself, however; then she felt better and accepted with cheerful smiles the little kindnesses the other girls ventured to offer her. She was soon prevailed upon to follow some of them out of doors and join them in play, and forgetting at the time that her playmates were deaf like herself, she began talking to them as she would to persons who could hear. This brought smiles of amusement to the faces of some; others shook their heads in a perplexed way, and still others acted as if they heard what she was saying, smiling and nodding their heads in a very knowing manner.

The morning after her arrival Carrie donned a neat new calico dress and was putting into the trunk the nice alpaca she had worn during her journey, when one of the older girls, who acted as special supervisor of the others, took it from her and, going to a large wardrobe, hung it upon a hook. Carrie objected to this, fearing someone would steal it, and she insisted upon putting it in her trunk; but the supervisor refused to allow her to do so. This so angered Carrie that she at once secured her hat and, declaring she would go home, glided past the supervisor and hurried downstairs and out of doors. The supervisor, who had followed the would-be runaway as fast as she could, succeeded in catching her before she had proceeded far, but she could not induce her to return. Soon the superintendent, who had been watching the scene from his window, came out upon the broad balcony, descended the steps, and came to the spot where Carrie, held an unyielding prisoner, stood. After some little time he succeeded, by his gentle manner, in inducing her to accompany the supervisor back to the house.

She had hardly reached the side door by which they must enter when Miss Tyndall, the matron of the institution, with an expression of great displeasure upon her face, came up to Carrie, seized her roughly by the arm, and administered a series of stinging blows upon her cheeks. From that hour Carrie both feared and hated Miss Tyndall. There are persons who can be rightly governed only by kindness, and who are made worse instead of better if severity is employed to correct them. Such a one was Carrie. Miss Tyndall, however, was one of that class who consider chastisement to be the proper remedy for all cases of disobedience, and thought she was only doing her duty in administering it. Carrie's actions seemed to convince her, however, that she had made a mistake in her mode of treatment, and she set about making amends for her harshness. Calling some of the other girls, she directed them to get their hats and accompany Carrie in a walk through the beautiful grounds of the institution. To this arrangement Carrie offered no objections, and the balmy air and charming autumn scenery, together with the pleasant manners of her companions, soon restored her cheerful spirits.

The next two days witnessed the arrival of many more girls and boys with bright, happy-looking faces. Their silent yet spirited conversation, and the play of varied expressions upon their countenances, proved for Carrie a source of much interest, though she kept shyly apart from the busy, animated talkers, aware of her inability to take part in their silent conversation.

4

The Commencement of School Duties

Thursday morning, the time in which active school duties were to commence, Carrie was placed with the other girls who stood in a long line in the large study room. After each one had been assigned a place in the line, they all marched in single file through the girl's sewing room, which adjoined their study room, and so downstairs and on to a large building adjacent, which they entered. Passing through a corridor, they mounted a flight of steps, at the top of which a door, to the left, led into the chapel, a spacious room, lighted partly by rows of windows extending along two sides of it, and partly by an immense skylight above. There were rows of long, dark-colored benches, commencing in front of and near an elevated platform, and rising gradually from it, each successive bench being about a foot above the level of the preceding one, thus affording a free and unobstructed view of the platform from remote parts of the room. Into this room the girls marched slowly, while through the door on the opposite side of the room a long line of boys were also slowly entering. After all were seated—the boys on the left and the girls on the right—a neatly dressed gentleman came into the room, mounted the steps of the platform, and, turning to the assembled throng, gazed into their pleasant faces for a few minutes; then, smiling, he made a few quick motions, which had the effect of bringing answering smiles to many faces. Carrie did not comprehend the remarks that produced this effect, but her bright eyes followed intently his every movement. Going to a small round table he opened a large Bible that lay upon it, turned the leaves slowly, then paused, as if reading. Next he took a crayon from a wooden box on the table, and going to one of a number of large slate stones, which were ranged along the wall on that side of the room, he wrote a few sentences. Laying down the crayon, he straightened up as if bracing himself for his task, and began a series of odd but graceful gestures, now and then stepping back a pace and drawing his finger slowly along underneath some of the words he had written on the large slate, then resuming his gestures. Presently he paused, stood a moment as if in quiet contemplation, then stretched forth his arms, with the palms of his hands opened and turned upward. At this motion all the boys and girls rose quietly to their feet, and stood gazing intently at him, while, closing his eyes, he again, but more slowly and with a certain air of reverence, resumed his silent and expressive gestures. Thus he continued for some minutes; then, bringing the palms of his hands together, he moved them slowly forward, and in obedience to this silent "amen" the boys and girls resumed their seats. Thus closed the first morning's service in the chapel.

The boys and girls now, class by class, filed slowly out of the chapel, going from thence to their respective schoolrooms to begin their tasks. Carrie was conducted into a large room. The first things noticeable upon entering this room—because of their novelty— were the large slate stones, in heavy wooden frames, ranged around two sides of the room. These slates, about two and a half by five feet in size, served the purpose of the common blackboard, to which they are far superior. There were about twenty of these slates in the room, designed for the use of the pupils. On another side of the room was a still larger slate for the teacher's use. A large double desk, with a row of chairs on each side of it, extended down the center of the room. This, with a small table and an armchair for the teacher, completed the furniture.

Upon Carrie's entrance she found a number of boys, apparently ranging in age from ten to eighteen years, seated along one side of the extension desk. She was shown to a seat at one end of the desk, and then discovered that she was the only girl in the class. Her new teacher—a gentleman not deprived of the senses of hearing and speech—had not yet learned the language of the deaf and dumb; therefore, he was assisted, at the beginning of his duties, by Mr. Hale, a deaf-mute gentleman of experience, as a teacher. Mr. Hale took a crayon from a box and wrote the word *cat* on the teacher's large slate; then turning to the class he pointed to the word with his finger and made a motion, as if pulling his mustache, with both thumbs and forefingers. Then he stroked the back of one hand with the other, in the same way that a person would stroke a cat's back. This was the sign for "cat." Next Mr. Hale wrote *cow*, and, closing all his fingers except the little fingers (which were held up stiff and straight), he placed his thumbs on either side of his head, thus making of his hands a sort of imitation of a cow's horns. Then he made the motion of milking. This completed the sign for "cow." The word *bird* was next written; and putting his thumb and forefinger to his mouth in the position of a bird's bill, he next spread out his arms, moving them to and fro in imitation of a bird's motion in flying. This was the sign for "bird." Writing the word *hog*, he placed one hand (the fingers of which were held straight) under his chin, and made a movement something like that made by a hog when rooting in the ground. Then he placed one hand high enough above the other, to indicate the size a hog ought to be. This was the sign for "hog." These strange motions made Carrie laugh; but she was afterwards to learn that all kinds of objects and also a great number of the words used in the English language were distinguished by some sign.

By this time the novelty of the gestures or motions had so enchained the attention of these new learners that they watched with ever-increasing interest every new motion, sometimes trying with creditable effort to imitate their teacher. But these motions were only the introductory step to the lesson. Having finished them, Mr. Hale took a book full of pictures of common objects, with which every child of ten years of age or over is supposed to be familiar. This book also contained many short sentences, and a few very simple stories relating to the pictures. Among the many pictures in this book he soon found one representing a cat. Then he pointed to the word *cat* on the slate. Next, book in hand, he went from one pupil to another, showing them the picture, sometimes stopping and pointing again to the word on the slate and then to the picture, to help some slow intellect to comprehend that the word was the name of the animal represented in the book. Some of the more wide-awake and intelligent among them looked at the picture for an instant, nodded their heads knowingly, pulled imaginary mustaches, and stroked one hand with another, showing thereby that they understood the relation of the word to the object. Each of the names of the other objects that had been written on the large slate was explained in the same way; but before this task had been quite accomplished the noon bell rang, and the pupils were dismissed to prepare for dinner.

After dinner a half hour was allowed for recreation; then the pupils were again marshaled into line and proceeded, class by class, to their schoolrooms for two hours more of schoolwork. In Carrie's schoolroom the forenoon's exercises were resumed.

When the time for closing school for the day drew near, Dr. Mayhews, the superintendent, entered the room and laid upon the teacher's table a number of paper-covered books. Each of these books—which were copies of the annual report of the Board of Trustees of the institution—contained, among other matter, copies of two alphabets for the deaf and dumb. One of these was called the "one-hand alphabet," and the other the "two-hand alphabet." Dr. Mayhews directed the teacher to distribute these books to the pupils, with instructions that they must commit to memory all the letters of the one-hand alphabet. "The two-hand alphabet," he said, "is not used in our schools, and therefore need not be learned by the pupils." The teacher, in obedience to these directions, distributed the books, and, with Mr. Hale's aid, explained to the pupils that they were to learn to form the letters with their fingers, as shown in the book. Then school was dismissed.

Carrie thought she would be free for the remainder of the day, but she was doomed to be disappointed; for scarcely was she out of the schoolroom when she was taken in charge by one of the older girls, who conducted her to the sewing room, where she found the other girls were assembling to take lessons in sewing. She was given a coarse linen towel to hem, and, sitting down on the bench pointed out for her, rather unwillingly began her task. Presently one of the girls noticed that she was sewing with her left hand. This fact was communicated to the seamstress, who came to Carrie's side, took the needle from her left hand, and placed it in her right one. Carrie took a few awkward, uneven stitches with this hand, and then defiantly returned the needle to her left hand and continued her work unmolested.

Thus the time passed until the small hand of the clock indicated the hour of five p.m., at which hour all needlework was gathered up and laid away, and Carrie, quitting her seat, ran swiftly downstairs and out upon the smooth lawn, where, with others, she indulged in pleasant and healthful pastimes until the supper hour came. The waving of a white handkerchief from one of the many windows signaled to some of those wandering about out of doors the fact that supper was ready. Those who saw the signal immediately, in turn, signaled to those who had not noticed it, and soon all hurried to the study rooms, where they took their places in line. Then came the march to the dining room. This being Thursday, the supper consisted of plenty of good, fresh bread, butter with just a hint of age about it, prune sauce, two cakes for each, and tea—the invariable bill of fare for supper on this day of the week. After supper another half hour was allowed for recreations, which were carried on indoors.

At seven o'clock p.m. all who were not already there were summoned to the study room, now brilliantly lighted by twelve gas jets. Here they took their accustomed seats at the many desks, and under the supervision of a teacher, commenced the task of preparing their lessons for the following day. Carrie laboriously formed with her fingers—all unaccustomed to the exercise—letter after letter of the one-hand alphabet until she came to the last one; then, after a short pause, recommencing the task, she with more ease formed them again. Thus over and over again the rows of quaint characters were repeated, until she remembered almost all of them. At eight o'clock p.m., she and the other small girls were excused from further study and conducted by a supervisor up to a large dormitory, which, with its soft, white beds, scrupulously clean, and its other neat appointments, looked very inviting. Carrie being tired, fell asleep in a very few minutes after she laid her head upon her pillow and slept soundly. She was awakened early the next morning by a gentle shake administered by the supervisor, and having, with some assistance, dressed herself neatly, she, with other girls, went below to a large washroom, where from a faucet she obtained cool, clear water with which she bathed her face and hands. Then, after combing her hair—for the performance of which she was obliged to borrow a comb, not having one of her own—she went to the study room. Soon the summons to breakfast came. This meal always consisted of bread, butter, hot coffee with plenty of milk and sugar in it, beefsteak—sometimes rather too tough—and gravy.

Breakfast over, the girls were sent upstairs to make their beds, which they were required to do very neatly. Then the various rooms, staircases, and halls were swept and dusted by girls specially chosen to perform these duties, while those otherwise unoccupied were sent to the sewing room to resume their needlework.

At eight o'clock the bell rang as the signal for all to prepare for morning service in the chapel. Work was then laid aside and, again, all repaired to the chapel to, "in dumb significants," thank God for the mercies and help already given and to plead for the bestowal of fresh mercies, strength, and help for the proper performance of the day's duties. Then the schoolroom tasks were once more taken up.

Carrie now had three new classmates of her own sex, who had arrived the previous day. The object exercises begun the day before were resumed. After a while a box of crayons was passed around, and the pupils were sent to the large slate blackboard to try to copy the words written upon the teacher's slate. This proved a rather awkward task for most of them, and the words they laboriously formed were but poor imitations of the neat characters on the teacher's slate; yet the teacher saw in them the germs of future success, and he smiled approvingly. There were some among them who were so unused to the task that after a few ineffectual attempts they gave up in despair, seeing which the teacher, to encourage them and teach them the proper way to operate, placed the crayon in proper position in the hand, which he then assisted to form the words. While thus proceeding on his round of inspection, giving a hint here and a lift there, he found Carrie awkwardly tracing the words in straggling, disproportioned letters on her slate with her left hand; and with a gentle remonstrance he promptly took the crayon from her left hand and placed it in her right. This new posture at first made her efforts still more awkward and difficult; but partly from a sense of duty and partly from the fear of being again corrected, she persevered in the use of her right hand, and gradually found the task of writing with this hand growing easier.

The day passed with the usual round of duties. The night hours, too, glided swiftly away, and with the dawn of Saturday morning the inmates of the institution again commenced their accustomed duties. At eight o'clock the chapel bell summoned the busy throng from their work to chapel devotions; again, when these were ended, did the boys and girls repair to their schoolrooms. Then the lessons studied Friday evening were recited. Carrie and her classmates were, one after another, called to the teacher's desk to repeat from memory the twenty-six letters through the medium of the one-hand alphabet. In the performance of this task some of them made but few mistakes; others could remember scarcely any of the letters. While these novices in language were exhibiting their newly obtained and meager knowledge of the "a, b, c's," other classes were receiving an outline of the Scripture lesson designed for the coming Sabbath. At ten o'clock a.m., school for the day closed and work was immediately recommenced, the girls going to their sewing and the boys proceeding to their tasks of learning trades in the cabinet shop or shoe shop connected with the institution, or in making splint bottoms for chairs, or doing odd jobs of work. Thus they continued until nearly noon, when work was stopped and all prepared for dinner.

Saturday afternoon was always a half-holiday, so many of the older boys, after their weekly bath, arrayed themselves in holiday attire, and with the superintendent's permission, wended their way to the city in search of amusement. The small boys and the girls both large and small were denied the privilege of spending their holidays in the city; so, after the indispensable warm bath, they were obliged to devise ways and means for passing away the time. Some of the more provident and tidy spent most of this time in repairing and arranging their wardrobes; a few read; some wandered aimlessly from place to place; some employed the time in writing letters; others played various games or engaged in conversation; and so the afternoon hours, one after another, slipped silently by. As the sun approached the western horizon the boys were seen—some alone, others in company—returning from the city; and by the time the supper hour came all had returned, tired and hungry and ready for the invariable supper for this day, which was bread, butter, cold beef, crackers, and tea. After supper all amused themselves as best they could until half-past eight o'clock, when all retired to rest.

5

Learning New Lessons

The sun shone out gloriously on Sabbath morning. It was one of those balmy Indian summer days that give one a delightful sense of rest and calm content. The gorgeous autumn leaves had begun to loosen their hold on the tall trees, and the slightest breeze was sufficient to send them fluttering tremulously to the earth. Carrie, who, with others, had gone out on the lawn to enjoy the fresh morning air, began darting about to catch these falling leaves, when one of the older girls, noticing her movements, reproved her gently and pointed in a solemn manner to the sky. Carrie looked puzzled, not understanding that the girl was trying to tell her that the Sabbath was God's day and should be kept holy. After a little persuasion, however, she was induced to give up her pursuit and allow the little crimson and yellow leaves to flutter unmolested to the ground.

Presently all the girls, now neatly dressed in their Sunday attire, were summoned to their study room, where an hour was spent by those who could read understandingly in studying a portion of the New Testament. The more advanced pupils had Bibles and question books for this purpose. Others studied their lessons from a book of simple Bible stories prepared for the deaf and dumb by an eminent instructor of the deaf in the State of New York, while those just started in their education simply studied the one-hand alphabet.

Almost immediately after the close of this hour of study, all the pupils repaired to the chapel, not to listen to, but to see a sermon delivered by the superintendent. The sermon ended, quiet walks or pleasant conversation filled up the remaining time till dinner.

At three o'clock p.m. they were gathered a second time in the chapel, and another sermon or lecture was delivered by Mr. Atwood, one of the teachers.

None of the pupils were absent from either morning or afternoon service, attendance upon these services being compulsory, except in case of sickness.

The afternoon passed quietly, no one being allowed to play or to indulge in weekday pursuits. The supper, at six o'clock, was the same as Thursday's bill of fare.

At seven p.m. the pupils assembled again in their study room for another hour's study. Slowly the hour hand traveled over the dial from the Roman figure VII toward the figure VIII. When that figure was at length reached, all were dismissed, and immediately they departed for the court of "Gentle Slumber," the queen of Slumberland, in the clime of Dreams.

The next morning, after breakfast had been eaten and the beds made, Carrie proceeded as usual to the sewing room. She had just taken her accustomed seat when a woman with a stern, determined demeanor entered the room, and, going to the seamstress, addressed a few words to her. In answer, the seamstress singled out a number of small girls, among them Carrie herself, and directed them to follow this woman. They obeyed. Proceeding downstairs and along a long, dark corridor, they came to a large room at the end of this corridor. Into this room the girls were conducted by the woman. Here they beheld, on long, linen-covered tables, great piles of pillowcases, sheets, towels, etc. To their dismay they soon learned that they were expected to iron all these articles. The woman proceeded to assign each girl to a place at the long tables, and then she pointed authoritatively at a large clothes basket—in which were a number of sheets already sprinkled and folded ready to be ironed—as the signal for them to begin work. Somewhat reluctantly Carrie did as the other girls were doing, secured a hot flatiron from the glowing stove at one side of the room, and set about accomplishing her imposed task. It proved a rather unpleasant task to her. It was required that not a wrinkle should remain in the articles, and that they should be folded with the utmost precision. This, to a novice in the art, was trying. The coming of the hour for chapel service released these girls for a while from this work, but as soon as school closed they were obliged to resume and continue it until every sheet, pillowcase, and towel had been neatly ironed and folded. They, by diligent effort, succeeded in accomplishing this before the hour when the girls engaged in sewing would be free, and they therefore gained a little more time for recreation that evening.

This being Monday, the supper consisted of a couple of warm biscuits for each person, bread, butter, molasses, and tea. This was, without variation, the bill of fare for supper both on Fridays and Mondays.

Tuesday morning about fifteen of the older and more experienced girls were sent to the ironing room, and, under the watchful eye of the woman in charge of this department of labor—who was quick to discover and reprove any carelessly done work—they used the flatiron sedulously, smoothing the linen of the officers and teachers.

Today Carrie and the other members of the lowest class had a new pantomime lesson, differing somewhat from all of their preceding lessons. Mr. Hale ventured to begin the task of teaching them words that represented actions. For this purpose he selected a few simple words. He took a crayon from the box and wrote the word *walk* on the large slate. Having pointed to this word, he walked across the floor and back to the slate. Then, to impress the meaning of this action more surely upon the minds of the pupils, he repeated it. Then stopping, he made a motion which suggested the idea that his arms and hands were walking on air. This was the sign for "walk." He next wrote the word *run*, and, as in duty bound, dropped, for the moment, his usual dignity and ran swiftly across the floor, much to the amusement of those who saw him. He supplemented this action by making his arms and hands perform the motion of swift locomotion, which was the sign for "run." After this he wrote the word *cry*, and placing the back of one hand over his eyes, imitated closely the actions of a small boy when crying. Then he made, with his forefinger, a motion suggestive of tears trickling down the cheeks. This was the sign for "cry." Next he wrote the word *love*, and pressed one open hand upon the other passionately against his left side, just over the heart. This was the sign for "love." The word *hate* was next written, and, with a look of disgust on his face, he made a motion as if to repel someone or something. This was the sign for "hate." The lesson was now considered sufficiently long for one day.

The day passed quietly with the usual round of duties. Tuesday's supper always consisted of precisely the same bill of fare as that of Saturday. The next day, which was Wednesday, another company of fifteen girls took their turn at the ironing tables to smooth out and do up the shirts of the boys, and so successive companies of girls were to be thus employed one day in each week, from Monday morning to Friday evening—no ironing was to be done on Saturday. In Carrie's schoolroom from day to day, the pantomime lessons representing objects, qualities, and actions were continued.

Carrie's teacher—Mr. Brown—by taking lessons in the deaf and dumb language from an experienced deaf-mute teacher after school hours, and by the aid given him in the schoolroom, soon acquired a fair knowledge of the deaf and dumb language and the method of teaching. He then was able to pursue his work in the schoolroom unaided. But he still continued to take lessons in the silent language every day after school hours. As time went on, repeatedly occurring events and incidents served to call into action and stimulate the once latent powers of some of the pupils' minds, which the daily pantomime lessons had awakened. They did not need much encouragement from the teacher to induce them to press on and make new investigations and new discoveries. They did so almost wholly of their own accord, often plying the teacher with eager questions. Others, with intellects dull of apprehension or indifferent to improvement, had to be constantly urged and helped forward in order to be able to obtain any knowledge of language. As the weeks went by and lengthened into months, Carrie became accustomed to the daily routine and discipline of the institution, and being quick of observation and tractable she improved rapidly.

6

Thanksgiving Day

The chill November days one after another passed uneventfully away until the twenty-eighth of the month. That day had been designated by the President of the United States as a day of national Thanksgiving. It was for the pupils at the institution a customary holiday. After breakfast they arrayed themselves in holiday attire, and at ten o'clock a.m. proceeded to the chapel, where a Thanksgiving discourse was delivered by one of the teachers. He reviewed some of the principal events of the past year and endeavored to impress upon his silent congregation the fact that they owed the many blessings they had received to the kind providence of God, who is the giver of every good and perfect gift. Finally all rose to their feet and stood in rapt attention while he, in silent language, returned thanks to God that all his unfortunate creatures at the institution had been so liberally provided for, had been kept in health, and enabled to enjoy many pleasures and privileges.

At the conclusion of the prayer the boys and girls repaired again to their respective study rooms in opposite wings of the main building. Their daily bill of fare for dinner, though not greatly varied, was wholesome and bountiful—usually consisting of fresh bread, boiled beef, gravy, two kinds of vegetables and pastry or pudding for dessert, with water for drink; but Thanksgiving dinner was always an extra affair. The coming of the dinner hour was, therefore, waited for with some impatience. At last everything was ready; each of the snowy tables was graced with a fat turkey and liberal supplies of vegetables, cranberry sauce, mince pies, etc., and the pupils were summoned to partake of the repast, which, after the usual returning thanks to God, they did with alacrity.

During the afternoon the girls, under the supervision of one of the lady teachers, amused themselves in various ways. Some, donning warm wraps, sallied forth for a short walk; others improvised waltzes and whirled with swift, graceful movements around the large sewing room, now transformed into a place for play. Still others engaged in quiet games, such as checkers and chess, and some of the more indolent indulged in an afternoon nap. The boys meanwhile also amused themselves in various ways.

The short afternoon drew swiftly to a close. The supper for this evening also proved an extra affair. There were in abundance bonbons and nuts, which were divided evenly and placed on the plates of each pupil; also apples, cakes, and honey for all. The supper over, after some delay the girls were formed into line and conducted through the grand central hall extending between the library parlors and reception room, into the boys' large study room. This study room, unlike that of the girls, was furnished with long, movable study tables. These had been pushed back into obscure corners and piled one upon another, to make room for the party in contemplation. Here, with some of the teachers to aid in devising amusements, a pleasant, sociable time was enjoyed until ten o'clock p.m. Good-nights were then said, and the girls conducted back to their study room, from whence they separated, going to their respective apartments. So ended this pleasant Thanksgiving Day.

7

Promoted

The following day school duties were again taken up and continued steadily through the succeeding three weeks, with no unusual occurrence to break the even tenor or arrest the daily routine of duties. The Christmas holidays were now drawing near, when one day Carrie asked her teacher this question: "When can I go home?" In reply, her teacher said, "You can go next Saturday if your father comes for you." That answer surprised Carrie very much, and when she communicated it to one of her classmates it was not at all believed. Not daunted by the doubts of her friend, however, she at once asked permission to write to her father, requesting him to come for her. Permission was readily granted, and, procuring paper and pencil, she sat down to compose her letter. She had scarcely commenced her task when the superintendent entered the room and, after exchanging a few words with her teacher, directed Carrie to take her book, pencil, and paper and follow him. She obeyed, wonderingly. Proceeding a short distance along the corridor, he stopped at the door of another schoolroom. He entered this room, and Carrie followed. As they came forward, Miss Mayhews, the teacher, paused in her work and, after a few words to her by the superintendent, gave Carrie a seat at one of the desks and supplied her with pen, ink, and copybook. Then it was that Carrie realized that she had been promoted to the class one grade above the one of which she had previously been a member.

The teacher gave her permission to finish the letter she had begun, and, forgetful of past admonitions, she grasped her pencil in her left hand, and without even the preliminaries of stating place or date, commenced awkwardly to scribble her petition to her father. The teacher almost immediately noticed the awkward way in which she held her pencil, and, going to her, placed it in proper position in her right hand. Holding it as best she could with this hand, Carrie succeeded in finishing her letter, which was as follows:

Mr. Mayhews will let me go home next Saturday if you will come for me. I want you to be sure and come the very next Saturday or it will be too late. I want to see you all so bad. Be sure and come.

Carrie Raymond

This letter she gave to her teacher to mail, who delayed doing so, in consequence of which it did not reach Carrie's father till Saturday night. When Saturday morning came Carrie was on tiptoe with expectation. She watched and waited anxiously for the summons which would tell her that her father had arrived. But as the day waned without bringing him, she sadly gave up all hope of spending Christmas at home.

The Sabbath came and quietly passed. On Monday morning the schoolroom duties were proceeding as usual when the nurse came to summon Carrie to the reception room, where, to her joy, she found her father, who greeted her warmly. Then he produced some beautiful presents he had brought for her. Carrie soon learned that Dr. Mayhews had given her father permission to take her home for a few days' visit, and she went to prepare to accompany him. While Carrie was getting ready for her journey home, Dr. Mayhews communicated to Mr. Raymond the news of Carrie's promotion, which much pleased him.

Very pleasant were the warm greetings Carrie received upon reaching home, and her short visit was to be both novel and refreshing.

Leaving Carrie enjoying the brief holidays at home, we will go back to the greater number of the pupils at the institution, who are obliged to remain there during the holidays. Let us see how their Yuletide will be spent.

8

Christmas at the Institution

Christmas morning dawned cold and bright. A deep snow had fallen during the night, and the bright eyes that looked out at the windows beheld a lovely scene. The limbs of the many evergreen trees that surrounded the institution were thickly covered with spotless snow, molded into many strange forms, while millions of tiny icicles and snow crystals glittered and sparkled like diamonds in the sunlight. These, combined with the smooth, white, glistening carpet spread over all the ground, formed a picture of such beauty as none but God, the creator of all that is pure, and good, and beautiful, could design or execute. "Christmas trees! Beautiful Christmas trees! *Many* Christmas trees!" said a dear little girl in rapidly executed signs, while her animated countenance told, in language almost as plain as her "silent words," the pleasure she felt as she stood at the window admiring the beauty of the outside world. Soon others came flocking to the window to gaze with her upon the grand winter scenery. Their delightful gazing was presently cut short by one of the other girls coming up to them and saying, "Hurry with your toilets. Breakfast will soon be ready, and you know the rules do not allow us to be late to meals." In response to these words, all began rapid preparations for the morning meal and soon were gathered around the breakfast tables.

At morning service, allusion was made by the superintendent to the time when the Savior of mankind was born, and wise men, beholding his star in the East, sought him that they might worship him; and how there suddenly appeared a multitude of the heavenly host praising God, and saying, "Glory to God in the highest, and on Earth peace, goodwill toward men." "That event," he said, "Christmas Day is designed to commemorate, and it is, of course, to be a holiday." This announcement was received with much satisfaction by the pupils. They then proceeded to their apartments to don their gala-day attire. The large sewing apartment was again arranged for a playroom, and the girls proceeded to amuse themselves in various ways until dinner was announced.

Upon entering the dining room they found a liberal supply of good things awaiting them. The feast was even more generous than their Thanksgiving dinner had been, and it looked so appetizing that many could scarcely wait till thanks had been returned to God for all his bounty. The slow process of carving of turkeys had come to an end before attacking the viands. At last, however, even the most voracious appetite was satiated, and all left the dining room in usual order. The afternoon was spent in various ways, according to the inclinations of the pupils.

The shades of evening gathering around brought the scattered population of the institution together once more, all radiant with the day's enjoyment, and soon supper was announced. Every plate at the long tables contained a liberal supply of toothsome sweetmeats. Besides the usual supply of bread and butter, there were dishes of honey, apples, and cakes, all so divided that each had an equal amount. The greater part of this meal was smuggled into capacious pockets for future enjoyment, the dinner having so effectually banished hunger that few felt like eating more.

Upon their return to the study room they were marshaled into line and conducted to the now brilliantly lighted chapel. As they entered, some looked inquiringly at the thick curtain extending from side to side of the room, hiding the stage from view, while others, who had before witnessed a like arrangement, sat in silent expectation with their eyes fixed on the curtain or curiously watched numbers of guests as they were ushered in and shown to seats. Quite a number of citizens, having heard of this proposed entertainment, had come, curious to know what kind of an entertainment the deaf and dumb could give.

It was not long before the curtain rose, presenting to view a beautiful scene. Kneeling upon a cushion, amid tasty surroundings, was a little girl clad in a dress of snowy white. Her long black hair fell in curls over her shoulders and shaded her face, most lovely with the beauty of health and innocence. Closing her eyes, she, in the beautiful language of signs, so silent yet so full of expression, repeated the Lord's Prayer. *Amen*, she silently and reverently said at the last, as she bowed her head. Then the curtain fell.

Next came a pantomime scene, entitled, "Which shall I follow, Religion or Pleasure?" When the curtain rose, there was seen to the right a young girl elegantly arrayed in a costume of gauzy pink tarlatan, with jewels gleaming in her hair, on her neck, her fingers, and her wrists. She was beautiful and represented *Pleasure*. To the left, beside a large, white cross, stood another young girl with hair of a golden tint that fell in curls over her shoulders. She was dressed in a plain, flowing white robe to represent an angel, or *Religion*. Between them stood another girl, younger and more beautiful than either. Her hands were clasped, and she seemed uncertain as to what she would do. *Pleasure*, with a winning smile upon her countenance, was holding up a roll of bank bills and jewels in one hand, while with the other she beckoned to the perplexed young girl to follow her. On the other side stood *Religion*, beside the cross, with an open Bible in one hand and a crown held out in the other. *Pleasure* beckoned gaily, holding her glittering jewels aloft enticingly, while *Religion* pleaded mutely. The young girl looked first at one and then the other, hesitatingly, for a few moments, and then went forward and, meekly kneeling, embraced the cross; *Religion* placed the crown upon her head. As *Pleasure* witnessed this, she turned away with a scornful smile, and the curtain fell.

Then came a representation, in two parts, of the four seasons of the year, given by four little girls. Spring was personated by a girl dressed in a gauzy, white costume decorated with bunches and sprays of artificial flowers, and she held in her hand a basket of flowers. Summer was represented dressed in white, adorned with flowers, and carrying a sheaf of grain. Autumn appeared likewise in a robe of white, carrying ripened fruits. Winter was shown as a girl in scarlet hood and cloak, holding in her arms a stick of wood. This was the scene presented to view in the first part. For the second part, these representatives of the four seasons were all arranged in line, and their burdens of flowers, grain, and fruit laid aside. When the curtain again rose, Spring, in silent language, recited a verse relative to that genial season. When she had finished, Summer, in turn, recited a verse appropriately fitted to the warm, glowing summer season. Next, Autumn recited a verse tending to bring to mind the glorious, though melancholy, autumn days. Then Winter, in her verse, told of ice-locked streams, howling blasts, snow-covered fields, and of the pranks of her ally, Jack Frost. Again the curtain fell.

Next came a declamation, delivered by a boy.

Then five little girls, ranging in age from eleven to thirteen years, took their places on the stage and delivered in voiceless language the following beautiful hymn, entitled

LOVE, REST, AND HOME

Beyond the toiling and the weeping
I shall be soon;
Beyond the waking and the sleeping,
Beyond the sowing and the reaping,
I shall be soon.
Chorus: Love, rest, and home—sweet home!
Lord Jesus, tarry not, but come.

Beyond the blooming and the fading
I shall be soon;
Beyond the storming and the shading,
Beyond the hoping and the dreading,
I shall be soon.
Chorus: Love, rest, and home—sweet home!
Lord Jesus, tarry not, but come.

Beyond the rising and the setting
I shall be soon;
Beyond the calming and the fretting,
Beyond remembering and forgetting,
I shall be soon.
Chorus: Love, rest, and home—sweet home!
Lord Jesus, tarry not, but come.

Beyond the parting and the meeting
I shall be soon;
Beyond the farewell and the greeting,
Beyond the pulse's fever beating,
I shall be soon.
Chorus: Love, rest, and home—sweet home!
Lord Jesus, tarry not, but come.

Three of these little girls would begin a verse of this hymn and proceed to the chorus, when the other two would join in this part. Their easy, graceful movements in concert, with no visible means of keeping time, surprised and delighted the visitors. "How is it possible for them to act in such perfect concert without even watching each other?" inquired one of the guests of the superintendent. He smiled, and answered, "Where there is a will, there is a way; and they have been well and carefully drilled."

There was now quite a stir behind the curtain for the space of about five minutes. Then it was again raised, and rather a woeful scene was presented to view. It was entitled, "The Woes of Bachelorhood." In a disordered room sat a man trying to thread a needle by the light of a flaring candle, but his efforts to force the thread through the eye of the needle persistently proved futile. As he sat there thus engaged, he presented a forlorn aspect. His shoeless feet revealed great holes in his neglected stockings. A torn coat, which he had undertaken to mend, lay across his knee; the worry and fret brought on by his ineffectual attempts to thread his needle had caused him to push his hair about in a very untidy way. He had almost given up his attempts in despair when, as if by mere chance, the thread went through the needle's eye. Then he took up his coat and began his task.

The first stitch would have proved all right had he not forgotten to tie a knot at one end of the thread. As such was the case, the thread slipped quietly through and separated from the material. Awkwardly tying a knot at the end of the thread, he recommenced his task. Two stitches were taken successfully, but the third proved too much for him. Having no thimble, he was attempting to force the needle into the cloth with his unprotected finger when the treacherous needle made a backward movement, forcing itself into his finger. With a look of agony depicted upon his features, he threw down his work, clasped the wounded member in his other hand, and began swaying back and forth. The curtain fell, enough of "the woes of bachelorhood" having been witnessed.

"The Lord Is My Shepherd" was next rendered in signs by one of the girls. Then followed prayer, by the superintendent, and the entertainment was at an end.

9

The New Year—Encountering Difficulties

The days subsequent to Christmas went slowly by. The old year, eighteen hundred and sixty-nine, silently, at the still hour of midnight, passed from the stage of being forever. The following morning, when the inmates of the institution awoke, they were conscious that the old year was dead and that a new year, bearing the title, "Eighteen hundred and seventy," was established in *his* place. Did they mourn for the dead year? No! The mind, in childhood, is inclined to enjoyment and not sorrow. It looks forward into the future, rather than backward into the past. Instead of lamenting the departure of the old year, they set themselves to work preparing to give the new year a pleasant reception.

After the gas jets were lighted on this first evening of the new year's reign, the boys were formed in line along one side of their large study room and stood awaiting the entrance of the girls. Presently in they marched, demurely, and formed in a long line on the opposite side of the room. Thus they stood for some moments until some of the more courageous and independent among the boys ventured to leave their places in the ranks and, crossing the room, solicited the pleasure of some particular maiden's company. Others soon followed their example. A few performed the civility of asking company with creditable politeness and grace; but the majority, having never studied etiquette and feeling rather shy and ill at ease, no doubt, stalked up to the girl of their choice and unceremoniously said, "Come with me." In some instances this invitation was promptly and peremptorily declined. Presently a quadrille was formed and danced successfully, even gracefully, by these silent people, without music or prompting. Waltzes were also danced, the dancers keeping time without the aid of music, as before. Meanwhile, those with quieter tastes had established themselves in cozy nooks and corners for games of authors, checkers, etc. Still others, of a romantic or talkative turn of mind, could be seen seated in some quiet place busily engaged in conversation and apparently oblivious of what was going on around them. As the evening advanced, games of "Blind Man's Bluff," "Snatch Partners," "Clap Out and In," etc., took the place of dancing.

Following this was a laughable exhibition given by several boys. They were furnished with large coffee sacks, into which they thrust themselves up to their waists, and, thus impeded, they all strove to see who could first reach a certain goal. The prize for the victor was nothing more than a large apple, yet the competitors all put forth their best efforts and strove with might and main to reach the goal first. But in the first attempt, all tumbled to the floor before the goal was reached. The competitors, however, got up and renewed their efforts until one sturdy fellow succeeded in winning the prize.

The fun and frolic continued with unabated zeal until the clock struck the hour of ten p.m. Then the superintendent announced that the entertainment must come to a close. This announcement brought out some expressions of dissent; but, in obedience to an order, the boys ranged themselves on one side of the room and the girls on the other. As there were some who could not reach the front ranks, the superintendent mounted a chair at one end of the room so all could see him. Attention having been secured, he asked, "Have you had a pleasant time?" The waving of many hands conveyed a hearty assent as the answer to this question. "Then," said he, "we must return thanks to God, who has made it possible for us to enjoy ourselves." All now stood gazing in reverent silence at him while he closed his eyes and, in the voiceless language of signs, offered up to God a prayer of thankfulness for his many blessings and his kind provision of means whereby the lives of the deaf and dumb are made happy and useful, and then he pleaded for continued blessings upon all. The prayer ended, good-nights were said, and with tired bodies but happy hearts all retired to rest, feeling secure beneath God's care.

The following day witnessed the return of those few who had been privileged to spend their holidays with loved ones at home. Among others, Carrie Raymond returned; and it was evident from her happy expression of countenance that she had enjoyed her visit home. The holidays now being over, all resumed their school duties with renewed vigor.

Carrie found her new duties rather difficult. She had to rely much upon herself and exercise her mental powers freely. Her teacher, Miss Mayhews, was in the habit of giving her pupils short stories to commit to memory, after which they were required to write them on the large slates ranged around the room for correction. This was no easy task for those with poor memories; but, with few exceptions, the pupils went into the work with hearty goodwill that promised success. After the completion of these stories—which were learned during the evening study hour and written in the morning—the class had a lesson in spelling. These lessons did not differ greatly from the spelling lessons in schools where the children can hear and speak, the only marked difference being that the teacher made the sign for some word instead of pronouncing it, and the pupil then spelled it by means of the one-hand deaf-mute alphabet instead of orally.

During the afternoon school hours the time was mostly spent by the pupils in endeavoring to improve in their penmanship. Carrie had now determined to learn to write well with her right hand, and bravely did she persevere in her efforts to accomplish this end. Sometimes the pupils were required to write little original stories from subjects given by the teacher. This was always a difficult undertaking to most of them—the proper construction of written sentences being to the deaf and dumb one of the most difficult parts of the naturally difficult task of acquiring an education. The chief difficulties arise from the fact that many of them are born deaf, or become so at a very early age, and therefore have no clear ideas of either spoken or written language. Their only language upon entering school, in most cases, consists simply of a few natural gestures. Not only are they compelled to begin at the very bottom rung of the "ladder of knowledge," but they also have to be awakened to the advantages and importance of spoken and written language. Everything taught must be conveyed to the pupil's mind through the eye or sense of touch. On account of these circumstances, an intermediate language that appeals directly to the vision must be employed to prepare the mind for the reception of knowledge, and thus they are to be led into a comprehension of spoken and written language. To meet that need, the language of signs previously spoken of is employed. That language is used by pupils almost wholly in conversation, even after they have learned the art of expressing their thoughts in spelling or writing. For these reasons the tendency is to write sentences much as they would express the same thoughts by means of signs.

In order that the reader may more clearly understand the nature of the sign language, so commonly used among deaf-mutes, let us take an example from a group of boys on the playground. They have learned the signs for various words in school and are now using them in a connected form of their own to express ideas. "Look!" a boy signs as he steps quickly to a companion's side, touches him on the shoulder, and points up at some object on a tree. "Bird little tree on see," he says in signs. Another just now notices a train of cars moving on the railroad some distance away, and says, "Cars go swiftly." Another, at whom someone has playfully thrown a snowball, says, "Ball-snow throw me stop!" Another has just peeped in at the bakery window and announces to his companions, "Pie-apple dinner," meaning, "We will have apple pie for dinner."

From the above it can be seen that the object present to the vision takes precedence over the other words of the sentence. This might naturally be expected when the first knowledge of a new language is conveyed to the mind through the organ of sight instead of that of hearing.

There is another peculiarity of the deaf-mute's mind which cannot be so readily accounted for. That is, the tendency to use the indefinite articles *a* and *an* in a wrong connection! Often they do not seem to be able to comprehend that *a* ought not to be used in connection with such words as bread, water, milk, etc., or that *an* should be used *only* in connection with the names of objects or qualities commencing with any one of the five vowels (*a, e, i, o, u*)! Thus such sentences as, "I eat *a* bread"; "a large horse drink *a* water"; "a bad boy steal *a* apple," are, during the first few years, constantly being written, even by those whom the teacher would expect to know better. When the mistakes are pointed out, the pupil's reply almost invariably is, "Oh, I forgot."

When Mr. Brown, who had hitherto taught his pupils only words, began the task of teaching them to write simple sentences, he did so without being aware of these mental peculiarities of the deaf and dumb. His first step in the direction of teaching sentence building was to explain the relation of various qualities to objects. This he did in the following manner without encountering any serious difficulties: Writing the phrase, "an old book," he took a tattered and soiled book, and holding it up so all could see it, he pointed to the words written. Next he wrote the phrase, "a new book," and held up a new book, pointing to the written phrase. Next he wrote, "a small boy," and placed a small boy in front of his desk. Then under this he wrote, "a large boy," and summoned a large boy to a place beside the small boy.

In order to give the pupils a knowledge of colors, he secured articles of different hues, and selecting an article of the color he designed to explain, he wrote the name of the article and the color of it. He then held up the article so that all the class could see it, and he pointed to the color and name written on the large slate. Next he selected another article of a different color and treated it in the same way as the previous article; and so on until all the colors of the rainbow, and others besides, were represented. Form, size, etc., he soon found could be taught in much the same manner.

He now went a step further. Writing, "I touch an old book," at the same time performing the action. He then asked, in signs, "What did I touch?" The pupils, who now readily understood the sign language, answered, "old book." He then wrote, "I open a new book," performing the action. Then he asked, "What did I open?" "Book new," or "new book," came the silent reply from various members of the class. After a few more examples of this nature had been given, he passed the box of crayons around and directed each one to write a few sentences upon subjects chosen by himself. The result looked so unpromising to him that he went to consult some of the more experienced teachers on the matter. In compliance with his request, two of them left their own work and followed him into his room. After reading some of the sentences written, one of the teachers said, "Oh, those are very common mistakes, and the pupils will do better by and by. It will require much perseverance and repetition on your part to enable them to effectually overcome some of the errors." Mr. Brown now began to realize more fully the difficulties of his work, and although driven at times almost to despair, he continued his attempts with commendable zeal and energy.

10

Some Glimpses into the Condition and Doings of Deaf-Mutes

One evening the superintendent brought some lady visitors into the girls' study room during study hour. After gazing around upon the neat, interesting-looking girls for a few minutes, one of the ladies turned to the superintendent and remarked, "How intelligent and attractive they look; and they appear to be happy, too, in spite of their misfortune. I always imagined that the deaf and dumb were much the same as lunatics."

"So they are, in some respects, when uneducated; but education elevates and refines them," replied the superintendent.

"Why do they make those quick motions with the fingers of the right hand?" asked the lady, trying to imitate the motions she saw the girls making.

"Oh," said the superintendent, "that is the one-hand deaf and dumb alphabet which they are in the habit of using to spell out each word while studying their lessons. It seems to help them to think; by using it habitually, they soon learn to spell words correctly from memory. Very few deaf-mutes are subject to errors in spelling after finishing their course of study."

"But," queried the lady, "how can they communicate their thoughts intelligibly to persons who do not understand the deaf and dumb language?"

"They can readily make themselves understood," replied the superintendent. "Would you like to have a demonstration of this fact?" he asked.

"Yes," replied the lady; "I am curious to know all about it."

The superintendent summoned a pleasant-looking young girl, requesting her to bring her slate and pencil. In obedience to this summons, slate in hand, she tripped softly down the aisle and, stopping in front of him, stood respectfully awaiting further orders. The superintendent, turning to the visitors, said, "This is Miss Grayson, a member of the class whose time at the institution will be out next year. She is both deaf and dumb. Please ask her a few questions and see if she does not prove herself competent to answer them intelligibly," he said, handing the lady the slate and pencil. The lady, smiling at her own stupidness in not thinking of that means of communication, yet wishing to make the test, took the slate and wrote several questions. She then handed the slate to the deaf-mute girl, who, after reading the questions written, took the pencil and in a neat, legible hand wrote the correct answers to them.

After reading the answers, the lady expressed herself as convinced of the ability of any intelligent, well-educated deaf-mute to converse readily with any person who knew how to write the English language correctly. "I am glad they can," she continued; "for I can hardly imagine a more pitiable condition than to be in full possession of intellectual powers and yet be unable to hold ready and intelligent communication with other minds."

Now, noticing how intently some of the bright-eyed little girls on the front seats were gazing at her, she asked, "May I have the pleasure of asking some of these little girls a few questions?"

"Certainly," replied the superintendent. "Susie, come here," he called, motioning to a little maiden, apparently about eleven years of age. Susie came forward demurely. "This little girl has been in school nearly two years," said he, "but owing to the great difficulties in the way of teaching language to deaf-mutes, she has not, as yet, learned to put words together so as to make correct sentences. She can, however, understand quite a number of simple words. Write,

'Bring me your book,' and see if she will understand and obey the order."

The lady did as he directed, and then handed the slate to the little girl. She took it and spelled out each word written, repeating the familiar word "book" several times. That one word seemed to give her an idea of what was required and, returning to the desk, she picked up her book and brought it, half hesitatingly, to the lady, who smiled approvingly.

"What is your name?" the lady then wrote. The little girl spelled the sentence swiftly and nimbly with her slender fingers, repeating the word *name*, which was also a familiar word to her; then confidently taking the pencil held out to her she wrote, "Eva Lane."

"Yes, that is her name," replied the superintendent.

"How old are you?" was next asked. "I am twelve old years," was the response. The lady smiled at the queer wording of the sentence. The superintendent informed her that this was a very common error.

Another little girl was seen busily writing on a slate, and the lady requested to see what she was writing. It proved to be a composition, and was as follows:

About a Rabbit

A tall gentleman went to a woods. He looked for the rabbit on the ground. He found the rabbit on the ground. He took his gun from his shoulder. He shot the rabbit. He put the rabbit into the game bag. He carried the game bag of rabbit home. He gave it to his mother. They very be glad it. She thanked him for it. She killed it with the sharp knife. She put it into the pan of water. She washed the rabbit. She put it into the large pan. She put the pan of rabbit into the oven. She took it from the oven, and she cut a piece of it, and she gave it to a little boy. He thanked she for it, and he ate it.

M. B.

The writer, the superintendent informed the visitors, was both deaf and dumb and had been under instruction three years. The ladies bowed adieu to the girls, who returned the civility with pleasant smiles.

It was almost the hour for retiring when the visitors withdrew, and those of the girls who, while the attention of the teacher in charge of them had been given to the visitors, had neglected their lessons to watch their movements, began studying industriously, justly fearing bad marks on the morrow if their lessons were not learned.

"Take this story to commit to memory this evening," said Miss Mayhews to her class on the following day, holding up the book opened at the story designated. The pupils took their books out of their desks and turned to the story. One after another they began asking the meaning of the words in the story which they did not understand. They spelled the words, and Miss Mayhews, by means of signs, explained their significance.

Penmanship was next taken up, and occupied the time till the close of school.

That evening, just after supper, the supervisor entered the girls' study room and, mounting a chair, proceeded to wave a handkerchief to call the girls around her. That signal being observed, and the girls also noticing that she held a sheet of legal cap paper in her hand, they came flocking around her, eager to learn the message she had to impart to them. After securing general attention, the supervisor said, "Those girls who have worked at prescribed tasks until now are relieved, and others here named are to take their places." She proceeded to give the new list of names, together with the special duty assigned to each. Their duties consisted of sweeping and dusting the various dormitories, halls, staircases, and other apartments on their own side of the building. The girls who had performed these tasks daily for the last three months were relieved, and they were jubilant over the fact. Some of them took occasion to express their satisfaction by a loud clapping of hands. They knew that their only duties for three months to come would be to assist in ironing one day in each week, sewing three hours five days out of the seven that go to make up a week, and keeping their beds and wardrobes in order.

After the reading of the list had been finished, and each one instructed as to what would be her especial duty, a number of the girls formed themselves into a ring and began one of their animated silent conversations. A hearing and speaking person, unable to understand this silent language if watching them then, would almost have envied them the ability and evident ease with which they conveyed their thoughts to each other without any danger of disturbing others or of tiring that very useful, though often unruly member, the tongue. But what were they talking about, do you ask? They were discussing the merits and demerits of institutions for the deaf and dumb in general, on the basis of knowledge they had gathered from various sources.

One girl who had spent some time in a western institution detailed an account of the various duties which were imposed upon the girls there. Said she, "In the morning, before breakfast, we had to tidy up our rooms. During meals, three or four girls, chosen for the purpose, waited on the others while they ate. The same number of boys waited on the other boys. When all the others had eaten, they were permitted to eat at the servants' table. After meals, about thirty girls assisted in washing the dishes, while others swept and dusted the halls, staircases, study rooms, dormitories, etc. Once a month, and sometimes oftener, we had to scrub some of the rooms, and every day, after school hours, we had to sweep the schoolrooms, or sew, or iron. But we did not have to iron the clothes of the officers and teachers as you do here. This was done by servants hired for the purpose."

"Did they pay you anything for your work?" asked one.

"No; we only received our tuition, board, and lodging as compensation, just as you do here. You have not near so much housework to do. You do not have to wash dishes, wait on tables, or scrub."

"No," replied one of the girls; "nor do I think we should be required to do these duties. With so many different duties claiming a part of our time and attention, our opportunities for obtaining a good education would be greatly diminished."

"I think," said another, "that it would be more profitable if the girls in all the institutions for the deaf and dumb were thoroughly instructed in cookery, dressmaking, tailoring, etc. Dishwashing and sweeping can be learned without a teacher; but one needs to be taught how to cook, bake, and make dresses and other garments in order to be able to do such work well. You know there are so few way for us to make a livelihood after we leave school. Teachers who can hear and speak are so often chosen to teach the deaf and dumb in preference to those who are themselves deaf and dumb; and we are also crowded out of other positions on account of our deafness."

The teacher on duty made her appearance at this point, and the girls were obliged to drop their conversation and begin the task of learning their lessons for the following day.

11

Easter Sunday

Under the influence of the genial atmosphere of spring, the snow had melted from the ground. Here and there could be seen little patches of green grass, while some of the many trees around the institution were covered with tiny buds, almost ready to unfold into leaf or blossom.

It was Sunday morning, and the girls tripping lightly downstairs and entering the dining room were surprised to see on all the tables dishes of boiled eggs. Then it dawned upon some of the more enlightened minds that it was Easter Sunday. The eggs were eaten with a relish, but with scarcely a thought of the event they were designed to commemorate.

The morning hour of Bible study passed, and then all repaired to the chapel for the customary Sunday morning service. As they entered and took their seats the attention of almost everyone was attracted to a number of beautiful hothouse plants, some of them in bloom, tastefully arranged on the platform. After admiring this unusual display, attention was turned to the Easter service, which was about to begin. This service did not consist in proclaiming by music and song, "Christ is risen"; there were no responses declaring "he is risen indeed." No; there was no music, no sound. In voiceless language the old yet ever-new, ever-wonderful story of the resurrection was told to the gathered throng, who, with bright eyes fixed intently upon the narrator, drank in the wondrous story of redeeming love and its triumph over death. This narrative was followed by prayer, and the Easter service was finished.

The boys and girls—some of them, no doubt, with new impressions of the glory and power of Christ—went from the chapel to their study rooms, where they engaged in pleasant, quiet conversation until the dinner hour came. After dinner another service was held as usual, but it was devoted to another theme. Softly, calmly sped the Sabbath hours away. One by one they silently came and passed, leaving behind no vestige of their presence save the record graven upon memory's tablets. The sun disappeared in golden splendor behind the western horizon; twilight shadows deepened; gaslight took the place of the departed light of day; swiftly moving fingers spelled out the lessons of truth and love from God's Holy Bible, some of which would live forever in the memory. The study hour passed; books were closed and laid aside.

The day, with all its events, was gone, never to return; yet thoughts of him "who hath swallowed up death in victory" and "is able to save to the uttermost all that come unto God by him," were to survive and gladden many a silent life. The reflection, "Jesus cared enough for me to die for me; and he has risen and gone again to his home in heaven, from whence he watches over me; and I know if I am good he will save me, and I will not be deaf and dumb in heaven," has power to cheer and help many of these silent ones when, as is not unfrequently the case, something causes them to feel bitterly their loss of hearing and speech. Ah, Jesus is indeed a silent comforter, one whom every deaf and dumb person should know, and, knowing him, they will love him.

12

The Annual Examination

As the term drew nearer its close, the pupils began to look forward with eager expectation to vacation and to count the months that must elapse before that pleasant season of rest and recreation should arrive. By and by they began to count the weeks instead of months, and as the weeks diminished in number, they counted the days. All this time everyone was very busy preparing for the annual examination, which would take place just before the closing of the term. That was an event which almost all dreaded, and as the time approached some trepidation began to be felt.

The day on which the examination was to be witnessed at length came, and the classes, with their teachers, the superintendent, and a few chance visitors, gathered in the chapel. The members of the lowest class were first summoned to the platform. Crayons were furnished them, and their teacher told them, in signs, to write their names and addresses. In obedience to that order they turned to the row of large slate blackboards ranged along the wall, and soon their names and places of residence were displayed. Some of them were written in quite a neat and legible manner, others in awkward, uneven characters, which, however, could be deciphered by most of those present. The teacher gave orders to his pupils to erase their names. Then, placing the first two fingers of each hand on each side of his head—to form ears— he moved them gently to and fro. In response to that sign the class turned quickly to the slates and wrote the word *horse*, that being the word the sign represented. A number of other signs representing various objects followed, the class writing with almost uniform readiness the names of the objects as they were represented. Next the teacher made the signs of various words and phrases, the pupils writing, as before. A few words were then given as the basis for short, original sentences. The sentences, when written, were short indeed, but some of them were very creditable, considering the brief time the writers had been under instruction. That class was excused.

The next class was called up, and when the members had ranged themselves in order in front of the slates and were supplied with crayons, their teacher gave them a number of words as subjects for original sentences, which they proceeded to construct. Some simple questions were next asked and answered in written form. That class was dismissed, and the next class called. They were first examined as to their ability to construct sentences correctly. The test showed some improvement in the art, although, as in the other classes just examined, some peculiarities of expression common to deaf-mutes were observed. Next they were given simple examples in addition and subtraction to work out. That was done correctly by most of the class. Then came some questions relative to Bible truths, which had been studied in a simplified form. After which the class was excused. The examination was then suspended for a time, and all withdrew to make preparations for dinner.

Upon reassembling in the chapel, the work of examination was again resumed, commencing with the class next in order to the class last examined. That class was chiefly made up of pupils who had been under instruction four terms of nine months each, or thirty-six months in all. Geography, which had been studied by the class in a simple, comprehensive form, was first taken up. Then followed arithmetic, and, after that, questions on Scripture truths, which had been studied in a simplified form, as in the case of the preceding class. Each pupil had also written a short original composition, which had been conveyed to the superintendent for inspection previous to the examination.

The next class called up was examined in United States history, geography, and arithmetic. Examples in addition, subtraction, multiplication, and division were given, as was a lesson in the Scriptures. That and other advanced classes were aided in their study of the Scriptures by question books embracing a series of lessons taken from the historical and prophetical books, the epistles, and the psalms, all arranged in order of time, with a brief, connected history of the Old and New Testaments.

As the examination of the classes proceeded, it was a noticeable fact that those who were the poorest scholars in written language could, as a rule, comprehend the method of working out an example in arithmetic more readily than those who were more proficient in language.

The classes that followed were examined in higher branches of history, arithmetic, geography, and physiology, and also in the Scriptures. These classes, three in number, all of different grades, had also written original compositions, which had been submitted to the superintendent for his judgment.

The examination—which occupied the greater part of two days—being ended, the superintendent, aided by the teachers, proceeded to make out a report of the standing of each pupil. That was done by filling out blanks in printed statements prepared for the purpose. These statements—which included a report of the pupil's average in examination, deportment, and promotion, if any had been made—were enclosed in envelopes bearing the names of the pupils to whom they belonged.

The following day, which was the last day of the term, the pupils, all dressed in their best, again assembled in the chapel, where they were joined by the superintendent and teachers. The classes were, one after another, called in front of the platform, where each pupil was given the envelope containing the report of his or her standing and instructed to take good care of it and show it to parents upon arrival at home. When the task of distributing these reports was concluded, the superintendent gave the pupils a few words of counsel, and then one of the teachers was invited to offer up a prayer. That being done, the assembly was dismissed.

13

Going Home to Spend Vacation

All was now life and activity, and preparations for going home were made rapidly. Trunks were packed, carried downstairs, and piled up on the sidewalk in front of the institution. The large farm wagons were brought around and soon heaped high with trunks of various sizes, capacity, and weight. They rolled away toward the Grand Union Depot.

Oh, how slowly the hours of that afternoon seemed to pass to the impatient throng awaiting the coming of the morrow, which would witness their departure for home—sweet home. They wandered aimlessly through the large, airy rooms, or strolled listlessly about the beautiful grounds, scarcely noticing how soft and green was the carpet of grass beneath their feet, or how lovely the trees clothed in their robes of living green. The thoughts of all seemed centered on the "dear ones" at home. *All* did I say? I should not have said *all*; for there were some who were homeless. On the morrow, parents of the fortunate ones would be waiting with eager expectation to greet their unfortunate children, doubly dear to them because unfortunate. How proud they would be to note the progress made in knowledge during the term. How gratified they would feel to witness their growth out of ignorance and helplessness into attractive, intelligent youths and maidens, or budding into respectable and refined manhood or womanhood.

But those homeless ones whose parents had died leaving them behind in the wide world! Who would welcome them? And who would rejoice over their progress? Were they to be entirely neglected? No! God has promised to care for the fatherless and to be a father to them; he had raised up kind friends for some of these homeless children, who would be waiting to welcome them and provide for their wants, while others were to be provided with places where they could earn their daily bread.

The longest and most wearisome day must some time come to an end. And so that long day, anon, drew near its close. Supper was eaten a little earlier than usual. After that meal—which was sadly slighted on account of the excitement caused by pleasant anticipations—was over, the pupils were divided into companies according to the route they were to take to reach their homes. Each company was instructed as to the time to be ready to start. One company, composed mostly of pupils living at long distances from the institution, was to leave that evening, and they at once began to prepare for the journey. Soon their good-byes had been said, and they were on their way. As the night came on, groups of girls gathered under the two solitary gas jets, which only dimly illumed their large study room, to engage in little chats; but the supervisor soon came into the room to bid them all retire to rest and gather strength for their coming journey. Some of them declared they could not sleep any that night, but, in spite of these assertions, "gentle slumber" visited every one of them.

Bright and early the next morning all were astir. Breakfast was soon served, and lunches for the travelers were prepared and brought up to the library. Company after company soon left the building and started down the street toward the depot.

Carrie Raymond had been informed on the previous day that her father would come for her and that she must remain at the institution until his arrival. She waited cheerfully for a while; but as one company of pupils after another departed, until the place was almost deserted, and still he did not come, she began to feel very lonesome and homesick. Noticing her dejected appearance as she stood in the library, Mattie Mayhews, one of the superintendent's daughters, asked, "Are you expecting your father?"

"Yes; but he does not come," Carrie answered.

"He will come," Mattie said, assuringly. But Carrie had now become rather despondent, and the tears would well up and fill her eyes in spite of her attempts to keep them back. Seeing that she was crying, one of the girls, at the superintendent's suggestion, led her away; but she refused to be comforted. "Carrie Raymond has been crying nearly all morning," said one of the girls to Miss Tyndall, the matron, who, by chance, came into the hall where Carrie was standing. "You must stop crying," said the matron, somewhat severely. That admonition was scarcely heeded by Carrie. A little while later the nurse, a kind-hearted little woman, with pock-marked face and hair arranged in the queerest fashion, came idling along in her usual spry manner, and, seeing Carrie still looking depressed, began talking to her, cheerily. She knew the cause of Carrie's trouble, and assured her that her father would soon come. "Watch for him," she said, wishing to give Carrie something to occupy her mind. She glided swiftly away to attend to some little duty. Carrie's spirits rose somewhat after hearing the pleasant talk of the nurse, and, stationing herself on a broad windowsill from whence she could see partly down the avenue leading to the principal gate, she proceeded to watch for her father. At length, after about half an hour more of watching and waiting, she discerned the lower part of a man's form as he came up the avenue. The overhanging boughs of trees prevented her from seeing more at that distance. But she felt sure, from the way the man walked, that it was her father; hurrying up to the nurse's room, she informed her of the fact. When they together, a minute or so later, looked out of the window, the man was in full view, and Carrie was not disappointed.

The nurse hurried her into the grand entrance, where she stood ready to greet her father. "We assured you he would come," said the superintendent, after Mr. Raymond had been ushered into the pleasant little reception room. Carrie's only answer was a smile. After a short conversation, Mr. Raymond, bidding Carrie remain a while longer, left the building in company with the superintendent and strolled down the pleasant avenue.

Presently Victor Walling, a pleasant-dispositioned deaf-mute young man, came up the steps to the portico, and, addressing the teacher with whom Carrie was conversing, said, "I have got a place to work this summer. I met a man in company with the superintendent, just now, who offered me a position at fair wages on his farm." "It was Carrie's father," replied the teacher. Victor Walling thought he was joking and expressed as much. Just then the superintendent came back and said to Carrie, "Victor Walling is going to work for your father this summer." Victor was now convinced and expressed his pleasure at the turn of affairs, and at once began to make ready to accompany Carrie and Mr. Raymond to their home.

The superintendent had ordered an early dinner for the travelers, but Carrie could hardly eat a mouthful. Mr. Raymond, who had gone to get a hack, returned in the course of an hour.

The superintendent stood beside Carrie, watching her happy expression of countenance as she put on her hat; and the dainty pink gingham cape that corresponded with her dress was fastened by Miss Tyndall.

"Are you glad to go home?" the superintendent asked.

"Yes," Carrie replied, with a happy smile. Good-byes were then said, and she tripped lightly down the broad flight of steps and entered the hack, followed by her father. Victor Walling entered a few minutes later. The driver closed the door, mounted to his seat, and the hack rolled away down the avenue and proceeded toward the depot.

It was dark when Carrie reached home, but her heart was full of sunshine. It seemed so nice to be at home with loved ones once more, and she had a beautiful home, too. The weeks of vacation were not long in gliding by; all too soon, thought some, the time for the reopening of school came around.

14

School Duties Resumed

The glorious autumn days, with their fading, dying splendor—fit emblems of the autumn of human life—once more had come. The spacious rooms of the institution, which had, during the three months of vacation, been silent and deserted, were again thronged with pleasant-looking boys and girls. The long and lofty halls once more echoed to the tread of many feet. Warm and loving greetings were exchanged between reunited friends and classmates, and a pleasant welcome was extended to every stranger who, as a member of the silent band, had come to claim the educational privileges of the institution. The chapel doors were once more thrown open for silent worship, and schoolroom tasks were resumed.

During vacation two new schoolrooms had been constructed to accommodate the increasing number of pupils. Two new teachers had also been added to the corps of instructors, both of whom were in full possession of the powers of hearing and speech.

Carrie Raymond, who had returned promptly at the opening of the term, was now placed in grade number three, under the instruction of one of the new teachers who had, from previous experience in another institution, acquired a fair knowledge of the language of the deaf and dumb. The studies designed for this grade were primary lessons in written language, geography, and arithmetic, and also the simplified Scripture lessons. Some changes were made in the school hours and also in those devoted to other duties. School now began a little earlier than usual. At ten o'clock a.m. there was a recess of ten minutes; then schoolwork was resumed, and continued until one o'clock, when dinner was served. After dinner there was no school; instead of returning to the schoolrooms, some of the girls repaired to the sewing room to use the needle and become proficient in needlework. Others were sent to the ironing room to wield the flatirons, and still others, to the schoolrooms, where, through the agency of the broom, they made the dust fly and the litter disappear.

Meanwhile the boys engaged in various vocations. Some of them were set to work to clear the dead leaves and other rubbish from the sidewalks and grounds of the institution; others repaired to the cabinet shop, where they engaged in the manufacture of wardrobes, tables, benches, safes for the storage of queensware, china, etc., and other articles of furniture; others resumed their places in the shoe shop to manufacture shoes for the poorer pupils of the institution; while others went to work to make splint bottoms for chairs. Visitors to the institution, on visiting the workshops, were surprised and pleased to note the degree of efficiency some of the boys had attained in the various vocations. Some of the articles turned out in the cabinet shop compared favorably with those of many manufacturers. These articles, too, sold readily.

A few weeks after the opening of school an incident occurred which will illustrate the deplorable condition of a person with an unawakened conscience. Carrie was one day, in company with several other girls, standing in the basement hall when two boys brought in an open barrel of apples. Carrie was very fond of apples, and when she saw the barrel brought in, she hurried up to it. The boys invited her and the other girls to help themselves to the fruit, which invitation they did not hesitate to accept. Carrie took half a dozen. A moment later the supervisor came down into the hall to divide the barrel of apples equally among the girls, giving two to each one as they, learning of the treat, entered the hall to receive a share. Carrie thought she would like a few more apples, and, as she chanced to have an uncommonly large pocket, she easily slipped the half dozen apples already secured into it unobserved, and then went up to the supervisor with empty hands and received from her two more. Strange as it may seem to some, this act of deception brought no feelings of compunction to Carrie's conscience at the time. This serves to show the insensible condition of many other minds.

Ah! The institution had a great and responsible work to perform in rousing the better natures of the unfortunate pupils and guiding their feet into the paths of peace and righteousness. The mind of a child is like a garden. We all know that if a garden is neglected, rank weeds will grow up and destroy its fruitfulness. On the other hand, if the gardener takes care to keep it in good condition and free from weeds, it will grow into a thing of beauty and utility. So the mind of a child, if it is neglected, soon becomes overrun with the poisonous weeds of sin; while, on the contrary, if by faithful, persistent effort, lessons of truth and righteousness are deeply implanted in the mind, it too will grow beautiful and useful. This seems to be emphatically true of the mind of the mute. Deprived as he is of one or, in many cases, two senses, the remaining ones seem to become all the more active; and this activity needs to be guided into right channels. The institution seemed sensible of this, and plainly, lovingly, and persistently, by word and deed, sought to impress the truths and requirements of the Gospel upon the minds of its pupils, thus to lead them slowly, it might be, but surely, into safe paths. Carrie was not yet in the safe path, as has been plainly shown; and it was well that she was under the molding influence of those who could guide her into it.

15

Dozing, and Other Incidents

Class number three, of which Carrie was a member, was, for a time each day after the morning lesson in geography or language, required to commit to memory a portion of one of the four arithmetical tables. Now, Carrie did not like arithmetic, and the mechanical act of repeating over and over, "once one is one, once two is two," and so on, or, "one from two leaves one, one from three leaves two," and so forth, and so forth, was very tiresome work to the little maiden. As she proceeded with the monotonous task, she would gradually lose consciousness of what she was doing and where she was. Her eyes would close and her head begin to bob in a helpless way from side to side, while her fingers struggled feebly to keep up their wonted movements in repeating and re-repeating the numbers. At this juncture the teacher's attention would usually be attracted to her, and she would be aroused. Although losing time by this involuntary dozing, she had such a ready mind that when the class was called to recite she could remember the lesson and write it without much difficulty. Carrie seemed to be naturally a "sleepyhead."

One day sometime after the incidents recorded above, she went into the study room after sewing hours and, pillowing her head on her desk, was soon fast asleep. When suppertime came the other girls either did not notice her or else did not wish to awaken her. After a while she awoke, feeling hungry. "Have you eaten supper?" she asked, as she saw the girls thronging up from the dining room.

"Yes," replied one of the girls, adding, "Have you not eaten?"

"No," replied Carrie.

"I am sorry," was all the consolation the girls could give her, for it was against the rules for anyone to eat after the usual hours, except under extraordinary circumstances. Going into the hall, Carrie met the nurse, who, as before stated, had a very kind heart. Speaking to her, Carrie said, "I was asleep, and no one awoke me; and I have had no supper." Upon learning this, the nurse tripped lightly downstairs, entered the dining room, and soon returned with a generous slice of bread spread with butter and preserved fruit, which she gave Carrie, bidding her go to some quiet corner, where she would be undisturbed, and eat it. Carrie obeyed, and so her hunger was appeased, and she felt grateful.

A strong friendship had sprung up between Carrie and Julia Keene, an orphan girl some years her senior. On one occasion Julia "took it into her head" to have her hair twisted around strips of tin, to make it curl. She informed Carrie of her intention, who, with the imitative tendencies so common in the young, concluded to follow her example. Accordingly they both secured a good supply of the "shining metal," and on Saturday night had their hair, lock after lock, rolled tightly around little strips of the tin. Then they sought their pillows, but there was not much sleep for either of them that night. Those little strips of tin proved such instruments of torture that anything like sound, refreshing sleep was out of the question. They arose in the morning with heads feeling quite sore, but still they were comparatively happy in the thought that soon their aching heads would be covered with numberless dancing ringlets. The little strips of tin were taken out, but the masses of hair, instead of curling, persisted in rolling themselves up into very unbecoming and unfashionable little puffs, between which little white paths wound in a mazy sort of a way. To remedy this, these little puffs were pulled apart, whereupon each individual hair seemed to have concluded to stand on end. The effect was much the same as that produced by the woolly locks of some of the African race. Of course the poor girls felt disappointed, but as they had gone to so much trouble and undergone a whole night's torture in producing this effect, they concluded to leave it the way it was for a while. Beyond some curious glances in their direction, and a few remarks upon their novel appearance, they were allowed to go unmolested. But the climax of their discomfort was not reached yet. This was to come when they attempted to comb out the tangled masses of hair, as they discovered upon making the trial. The strong teeth of their combs could scarcely be forced through the tangled, bristling wilderness of hair. Their heads, made tender by their night's experience with the strips of tin, were made still more so by the hard pulls necessary to untangle the stubborn locks. Julia, in her attempts, broke her comb; and it took almost an hour's work to untangle and restore the hair to its natural condition. This experience, it is hoped, proved a lesson to both of the girls.

In due time Thanksgiving Day came round again, and was celebrated in much the same way as it had been the previous year.

Time, which never pauses or tarries even for an instant, passed silently onward. The Christmas holidays again drew near, and Carrie, unauthorized, wrote to her father, saying, "Mr. Mayhews will let me go home on the eighteenth day of December to spend Christmas, if you will come for me." On the day designated, Mr. Raymond arrived at the institution, but there was a shade of displeasure in his face as he greeted Carrie, which she could not at first account for. Presently Dr. Mayhews spoke to her, saying, "Did you write to your father telling him that I would let you go home on this day of the month, if he came for you?" Carrie acknowledged that she did. "It was wrong of you to do so without consulting me; and I think I must punish you by not allowing you to go home," said Dr. Mayhews.

A look of surprise and disappointment came into Carrie's face. She had thought it would be all right, as she had not consulted him the previous year, and he had readily allowed her to go; but, of course, the time then was a week nearer Christmas Day. Dr. Mayhews saw Carrie's look of disappointment and, after some deliberations, relented and concluded to let her go home, feeling that she would enter more heartily into her schoolwork after a few weeks' recreation. "If it were possible," he said to Mr. Raymond, "we would like to give all of the pupils a chance to spend the Christmas holidays at home, but the expense, etc., for many of them would be so great that it is not practicable. We always endeavor to make the holidays pass pleasantly to those remaining at the institution." As Mr. Raymond was leaving, he said, "Bring Carrie back immediately after New Year's Day. We do not wish her to lose any lesson that might be helpful to her or to fall behind her class." Mr. Raymond promised compliance with this request and departed, taking Carrie with him.

Christmas, the day always eagerly looked forward to by the inmates of the institution, was once more very near, and the steward's wagon, upon his daily arrival from the city, usually contained boxes of presents to make glad the heart of some boy or girl. These boxes were seized and borne away by the happy owners, who were soon rejoicing over their contents, feeling very grateful to the dear ones at home who had so kindly and generously remembered them. Christmas Day, this year, was spent very much as on previous occasions, as was also New Year's Day. Then the few who had spent the holidays at home returned, and school duties were cheerfully taken up once more.

16

Some Unexpected Events

Some weeks after the holidays had passed, Miss Carver, Carrie's teacher, was surprised when, upon entering her schoolroom as usual one morning, she found it tastefully decorated with festoons and wreaths of evergreens. She was at a loss to understand what had led to the sudden transformation of the room and whose work it was, until one of her pupils informed her that they had done it in honor of her birthday. Then it suddenly occurred to her that it was indeed her birthday. In a very pleasant manner she thanked the class for this token of their appreciation of her work; then she asked, "But how did you know it was my birthday?"

"I asked you a long time ago, and you told me then," answered one little girl.

"Oh, I had forgotten," said Miss Carver. "And so you wanted to know in order to surprise me," she added, laughing. "Yes," was the reply. But the surprise was not yet at an end. Presently the door of her schoolroom was opened and in came the only absent member of the class, followed by the members of the highest class. Each person, upon entering the schoolroom, shook hands with Miss Carver and passed up one of the side aisles of the room to give place for others. After all had entered and greeted Miss Carver, a few moments were spent in inspecting the decorations, and then they departed for their own schoolroom. Scarcely had they gone, however, before another class filed into the room, and the same ceremony was again enacted. And so class after class came, from the highest down to the lowest grade. This unexpected reception, in which both teachers and pupils joined, soon came to an end, and all once more resumed their school duties.

About this time, some of the members of the state legislature and other persons visited the institution, and, after they had inspected different parts of the buildings, the pupils were all summoned to the chapel, where an exhibition of a miscellaneous character was given for the benefit of the visitors. Members of the different classes were called up to write, and thereby show, the progress being made in language and in the various studies. Then two boys enacted a story entitled "Fishing." This was done by means of natural motions, which even those not familiar with the deaf and dumb sign language can readily understand. Next Mr. Vance, a deaf and dumb teacher possessing excellent imitative faculties, told in the same natural motion-language, a story of a man shaving while being watched closely by a monkey, which, when the man left the room for a moment at the close of the operation, seated itself upon the bureau and proceeded to lather its own cheeks, as it had observed the man to do. But the poor monkey, not being careful, got some of the lather in its eyes, producing an agony of pain. Dropping the brush, it plunged its paws into its smarting eyes, trying vainly to allay the pain, at which point the man reappears upon the scene. These and other stories were strongly applauded by the visitors, showing that they appreciated them. The pantomime language in which they were delivered differs from the ordinary sign language of the deaf and dumb, being simply imitations of various actions of persons or animals. Some deaf-mutes possess the faculty of imitating other people's actions, and also the actions of some animals, to a surprising degree. This, no doubt, is owing to the fact that they are close observers of what is going on around them.

There is another, though not distinct, phase of the deaf-mute language in which some show great proficiency. This is the expression of the various emotions of the human heart by look or action. In connection with the sign expressing joy or happiness, the countenance lights up with a happy smile. When making the sign for "hope," a look of expectancy accompanies it. In expressing trust or faith, a peculiar look of peaceful reliance comes into the eyes, and if it is an expression of faith in Christ, the eyes are raised heavenward. The sign for "anger" is accompanied by a scowling or angry look. Along with the sign for "sorrow" comes a sorrowful or sympathetic expression. Fear is expressed by trembling of the limbs and looks of terror. In "doubt," an expression of disbelief is depicted upon the features. Shame is expressed by hanging the head and assuming a humiliated appearance. The sign for "scorn" is accompanied by a look of contempt. Pride, or vanity, is portrayed by strutting pompously across the floor. Love and hate have previously been depicted. Emphasis, indecision, weariness, despondency, etc., are also shown in much the same way as the emotions just described.

At the close of the exhibition above mentioned, one of the visiting gentlemen arose and addressed the silent throng, expressing himself as much pleased and somewhat surprised at the degree of intelligence and improvement manifested. The visitors then left, and the classes returned to their respective schoolrooms.

One pleasant Sunday morning a minister of the Episcopal Church came out to the institution to preach to the pupils. When, in company with the superintendent, he mounted the steps of the platform to begin the service, he was arrayed in the long white robe known as a surplice. Many of the pupils had never before seen a minister thus arrayed, and looks of amusement or astonishment were depicted upon the countenances of some of them. The minister probably noticed this, for he directed the superintendent to explain to them that it was customary for ministers of the Episcopal Church to wear this robe when holding religious services. This explanation was satisfactory, and all gave attention to the service, which was translated into the deaf and dumb language by the superintendent as fast as it was delivered in spoken language by the minister. Among other things, he related a sort of a parable, which was as follows:

> A prize was offered by a great King to all who reached a certain goal before the close of day, at which time, a great gong would strike announcing that the chances of winning the prize had gone by. Three persons learning of this prize, and the conditions upon which it was to be obtained, set out to reach the goal and win it. Two of them were strong and active, unencumbered by any great hindrances; but the third was lame. The two whose limbs were strong and whole thought there was no need to hurry, and as the sun was warm and bright, and everything looked so pleasant, they loitered along the way, culling the beautiful flowers, or feasting on the luscious fruits that grew at some distance from the path. But the lame person, knowing well the lack of power in himself, pressed right onward, never stopping to indulge in the pleasures held out to him on the way, yet able to enjoy, as he went along, the beautiful scenery, and the singing of the birds overhead. Meanwhile the other two had become quite oblivious of the lapse of time, so absorbed were they with the pleasures of the way. The sun sank lower and lower, while the lame person, though grown weary with the heat and burden of the day, toiled on, each successive step bringing him nearer the longed-for goal. The two whom he had left loitering along the way by and by became conscious that the day was nearing its close and that they must put forth their best endeavors in order to reach the goal before the sun went down to dawn upon no hopeful tomorrow, and the fatal gong should sound. Without further delay they prepared to press onward to the goal, but found they had not strength enough left to enable them to reach it. On the contrary, the lame person, whose chances at the outset were so small and unpromising, had,

by steadily and perseveringly pressing forward, reached the goal, won the prize, and was fully satisfied.

"The great King," concluded the minister, "is God. The prize he offered, and still offers, is eternal life. The day signifies this mortal life. The gong sounding is death. The prize is offered to every one of us who will strive to win it. Let us, then, 'press toward the mark for the prize of the high calling of God in Christ Jesus.'" An impressive prayer now closed the service. It had been followed intently by the keen, bright eyes of the pupils, which truly seem to possess greater visual powers than the eyes of persons who can hear.

We cannot tell how much of real good this simple sermon accomplished, or how many of these silent ones took its lesson home to their own hearts; but we believe that every earnest, unselfish effort to help on the interests of God's kingdom does some good. Often the work of instructing the deaf and dumb in spiritual things—things that cannot be perceived by the natural eye—seems like attempting to impart knowledge to dumb, inanimate things. But if the instructor proceeds with his work as best he knows how, relying on God for help and trusting him to crown the efforts with success, the good results will certainly appear in after years. This fact has been verified over and over in the after lives of many pupils, the good seed having not been sown in vain, though it had long laid dormant in the mind.

The winter months passed profitably and pleasantly away, and once more March came round on his annual visit to our globe. He seemed to be in excellent spirits this year, for his usual blustering manner was lacking, and his smile was very genial.

One day, at the close of their school duties, as the girls were slowly wending their way toward the large main building, the attention of some of them was attracted to an unusual sight in front of the building. A sort of covered shed had been erected, and at a little distance from this were several men standing around some object. Curious to know what this object might be, they began to venture near the group. The superintendent, who was among the men, noticed their approach and signaled to them to come nearer. They obeyed and came thronging up to him in full force. Soon he had them all grouped together near a cluster of large forest trees, and before it was clear to some of them what all this meant, they were having their photographs taken, along with the main building, upon which the photographer's camera had already been directed. Some among this photographic group presented an amusing appearance when the work was finished. Some of them, in lieu of bonnets or hats, had opened their schoolbooks and placed them astride of their heads to keep off the beams of the sun; others had, apparently for the same purpose, made turbans of their handkerchiefs. The various attitudes assumed seemed intended to suit their own comfort and convenience rather than the artist's fancy; yet all appeared to consider it an honor to have had their own pictures taken in connection with the imposing structure known as the institution for the deaf and dumb.

17

A Picnic, and How It Ended

As May approached, the superintendent decided to give the pupils a holiday and allow them to spend it in the woods some three miles away. Accordingly, one sunshiny May morning the light-hearted boys and girls emerged from their school home and wended their way through the beautiful grounds, over grass that was fresh and green. The sunbeams that found their way through the masses of foliage down to Mother Earth seemed dancing gleefully, as if they, too, were enjoying a holiday.

The long procession passed through the great iron gates and followed the dusty highway which led toward the cool retreat whither their feet were bound. Immediately upon reaching it, they scattered in different directions, some, in groups, going in search of the wildflowers which may be found only in the wildwoods, and others to look for the many curiosities that abound there. The search was well rewarded. Soon the scattered companies began to return to the place selected for the rendezvous, many with hands filled with beautiful but fragile flowers, ferns, acorns, and the like.

The walk through the dim forest aisles, where the tall trees lifted their heads majestically heavenward as monuments of the power and skill of their great and good Maker, and where the little wildflowers and tiny blades of green grass seemed silently speaking of his thoughtfulness and care for even the smallest and apparently most insignificant things that he has made, evidently had done them good. All were in excellent spirits.

A swing was put up, and soon some of the girls were being swayed back and forth, now ascending high into the air, now sweeping gracefully down to earth again, their smiling faces betokening their enjoyment.

Meanwhile a number of the boys, having found a suitable plot of ground, engaged in playing a game of baseball, while others watched the sport, entered into conversation, or strolled about from place to place. After a while some of the less generous boys insisted that they ought to have the use of the swing, and the girls surrendered it to them—not very willingly, however.

Toward noon some of the teachers who were in full possession of the sense of hearing and who had accompanied the pupils to the woods to enjoy with them the holiday, heard peals of thunder. Justly fearing the approach of a thunderstorm, the picnickers were hastily arranged in marching order and, led by a teacher who had grown old in the service of the deaf and dumb, they started for their stronghold—the institution. Scarcely had they left the woods and struck out into the highway before the storm burst upon them. It was opened by the flash and roar of heaven's artillery, the loud vibrations being felt by the strongly sensitive among these silent ones. At this crisis they broke rank, left the road, scrambled over a high rail fence, and used their feet to good advantage—hurrying across the field like a flock of frightened sheep.

Carrie ran on and on, now and then looking up at the black and threatening sky as a flash of vivid lightning darted athwart the dark mass of clouds that shut out every trace of the calm blue sky which had greeted the gaze that morning. She uttered a silent prayer to God, whom she had begun to recognize as the maker and ruler of all the vast universe, and the one who alone could protect in such a time of danger.

Her breath began to grow labored from her rapid running, and her limbs were so tired that she hardly hoped to reach the school unaided. But still she was enabled to speed on and was gratified to know that every step brought her nearer to a shelter from the storm. The high picket fence that surrounded the institution was reached. A few pickets had been torn off, to afford an entrance, and through this narrow gateway the throng was passing. Carrie had, in order to protect her hat from the rain, wrapped it up in her white apron, and after she had crept through the narrow entrance she began to feel a weight upon her head. Putting up her hand to ascertain the cause of this, she found a man's hat. She was at a loss to know how she came to be wearing this hat, but supposed it must have been put on her head by the gray-headed teacher whom she saw standing by the opening in the fence as she crept through, looking solicitous for the welfare of the unfortunate picnickers. Hailstones, like mimic bullets, began to patter down upon their defenseless heads, but the institution was almost reached. The superintendent stood in a side door with a look of anxiety upon his kindly face as the drenched and forlorn-looking figures came thronging up.

They entered this door and passed upstairs into the boys' study room. Here Carrie took the heavy black hat—which had so unexpectedly come into her possession—from her head, and laid it upon a table. Then she followed the other girls, who were proceeding through the long halls toward their own apartments. The strength of one or two had given out on the way, but stronger ones lent them a helping hand until they had reached the institution in safety.

After the wet garments had been exchanged for dry ones, a bountiful dinner eaten, and cups of hot tea drank, all felt quite cheerful and disposed to laugh over their adventure.

In the afternoon several of the girls who had not undertaken to run across the fields in the storm, seeking shelter in a private house instead, made their appearance, dry and comfortable. Beyond the general weariness and discomfort felt, no harm resulted to anyone. God had signally illustrated his omnipotence, and at the same time shown his mercy and loving kindness.

A few days later Carrie's father came to visit her, and of course he was given an account of the picnic. He was next shown some copies of the photograph of the institution taken with the girls grouped in the foreground, and was so pleased with it that he bought a copy. Before he left, Carrie gave him her hat to take home to the milliner, to be remodeled and retrimmed, requesting him to send it back to her before the close of school, as she would need it to wear home.

18

Closing Exercises of the Term

Each year, it was the custom to allow those who completed the course of primary study with more than the average success the privilege of remaining for more than the prescribed number of terms and receiving a higher education. This consisted of a three years' course, including advanced lessons in geography, grammar, arithmetic, rhetoric, physiology, philosophy, chemistry, and algebra. This term a class of five persons—two young gentlemen and three young ladies—would complete this three years' course of study and receive diplomas. Preparations for the graduating exercises had been in progress for some time. The original essays which they had been required to prepare for the occasion had been written, and the writers, by daily practice, were trying to acquire a graceful and easy style of delivery.

Preparations for examination were also being made. This year, as the superintendent announced one morning, the examination was to be conducted in a different manner from that of the preceding year. The graduating class and the higher primary classes were to write the questions given them by their teachers, and also their own answers to these questions, on sheets of notepaper furnished for the purpose. Twenty-five questions in each study pursued during the term were to be asked and answered.

Meanwhile the lower primary classes were to be examined under the eye of the superintendent, in much the same way as the previous year. There were some who did not like the idea of having every item of their examination on paper, but the decrees of the superintendent, which were wise and judicious, must be obeyed. There was only one sure way to conquer this dislike, and that was to be so thoroughly prepared for the work as not to fear the results. Some of the pupils sensibly resolved to study still more diligently than they had been doing and to fix the hard lessons firmly, right side up, in their minds. But others—and these were the more numerous—being disinclined to make any great exertions, and apparently thinking that knowledge was not worth the winning if there was no "royal road" to it, concluded that they need not try to pass a very creditable examination. So they went over their lessons in a manner of easy indifference that did not promise to bring them very high-credit marks. Thus they allowed the time to glide by, and, almost before they were aware of it, the day upon which examination was to be begun had arrived.

After the service in the chapel had ended on the morning of this particular day, the classes proceeded to their respective schoolrooms. After some hasty glances over the pages of textbooks, taken by some of the pupils in order to fix some principles of knowledge more firmly in memory, the books were all gathered up and laid away, and slates, pens, ink, paper, etc., were arranged ready for use.

The teachers, in their different rooms, then began simultaneously writing selected questions to be answered. Meanwhile anxious eyes read each question as it was written, fearing lest some puzzling question, the answer to which might have slipped the memory, should be asked. A sense of relief was felt when question after question proved to be such as could be answered correctly. But as the work advanced, almost everyone met with difficulties, some giving up the attempt to answer certain questions in despair; others, after close thought, happily recalling the correct answers.

The examination of some of the classes extended through three or four days, while that of others was completed in less time. The examination papers were conveyed to the superintendent, who, in turn, conveyed them to the examining committees composed of the teachers, who read each one and marked it according to the number of mistakes made. A perfectly correct paper was marked 100. When one mistake was discovered, and no more, the paper was marked 99; and so on. Some of the examination papers showed quite commendable results and were evidence that the writers had studied diligently and taken care to do their work well. Others were almost equally censurable—manifesting, as they did, a lack of care and close application. At last all of the large number of papers had been read, and the mistakes noted down. Next came the work of making out reports of the standing of pupils. This was done in a manner previously stated.

Very near the close of the term all the pupils enjoyed a pleasant social party, at which strawberries, cakes, and candy were served and partaken of with great relish.

Then came what was, to some, the most momentous event of the term—the graduating exercises. The pupils, and a number of visitors, upon entering the chapel on the morning when these exercises were to take place, found the candidates for academic honors seated in a row on the platform. The ladies were all dressed in white, with small bouquets of gay-colored flowers fastened at the waist; in their hands they each held a lovely bouquet of flowers fresh from the greenhouse. The gentlemen were dressed in black, with gay buttonhole bouquets displayed on the coat lapel. Each had also been presented with a large bouquet of cut flowers.

The exercises were opened by a short address from the superintendent. The name of the lady who was to lead in the exercises was called, and she arose from her seat, advanced a few steps, bowed—first to the superintendent and then to the assembly—and then, with the fingers of her right hand, she spelled out her subject and proceeded in signs to convey the thoughts of her essay to the minds of the silent throng. Meanwhile her teacher, standing in front of the platform, translated the silent language of signs into the vocal language of speech.

That essay ended, the young lady again bowed to the assembly and resumed her seat.

The name of one of the gentlemen was next called, and, rising from his seat in obedience to the summons, he took one or two long strides forward, made a motion of greeting, first with one hand and then with the other, in order to include the whole of the assembly. This motion of greeting, by the way, is much like throwing kisses, and has sometimes been mistaken for that by persons who do not know the deaf and dumb sign language. But it is used by the deaf and dumb only to express "good day," "how do you do," and kindred greetings. A sign almost similar to it is employed to express "thanks."

After this greeting he spelled out the subject of his address, and then in ponderous signs delivered it, the teacher, as before, translating the signs into spoken language.

When he had finished and taken his seat, the name of another lady was called. As she arose, it was noticed that she was above medium height; and the erect manner in which she held herself made her appear very tall. She bowed, first to the superintendent and then to the assembly, as the other lady had done. She then carefully spelled out the subject of her composition, and in graceful, comprehensive signs gave the thoughts contained in her theme.

Next came the other gentleman's turn. When his name was called he came forward quietly, gave the same sort of a greeting as the former gentleman had done, and proceeded with his essay in the usual way.

The remaining lady—the last of the number—was next called. Like the lady last referred to, she was also above medium height, and she had a rather haughty bearing. There seemed to be a tinge of *hauteur* even in her manner of delivering her essay.

When she had resumed her seat, the superintendent arose, and, requesting the candidates to rise, he addressed them in a few parting words of friendly counsel and encouragement, reminding them that their time in that school was at an end, and that they were about to leave its shelter and go their way out into the wide world. He begged them to remember the good lessons they had learned while there and to try to profit by them. "You may meet," said he, "with trials and temptations; but try always to do right, trusting God constantly for strength and guidance." Then he commended their efforts to acquire an education and spoke of the happy results. After that address he presented each with a diploma.

The graduating exercises were now at an end, and the work of giving the reports of standing to each of the other pupils was commenced. That ceremony being ended, prayer was offered in which blessings were invoked for all, and the assembly dispersed.

The afternoon was spent in making preparations for the homeward journey. The thought of again beholding the loved ones at home filled many hearts with joy. Today there seemed to be no theme which they considered worthy of discussion save that of home and home pleasures. It has been truly said, "There is no place like home, be it ever so humble." Especially is the truth of this felt by children. Happy are they, then, if their homes are made bright and beautiful by God's Holy Spirit ruling in the hearts of the household. Such homes are as the gate to the beautiful home in heaven, which is lighted by the glory of God and of the Lamb. It is sad to think that all have not such homes. Some of them live in homes whose doors are never opened to God's Spirit—in which there is no place reserved for the pure and loving Jesus, no hour devoted to his service. Such homes must always have a gloom hovering over them. There can never be so much heartfelt joy and real happiness in them as in the homes where Jesus is always an honored and often-present guest—nay, more, a constantly abiding presence.

It need not be thought strange if children, brought up in homes from which God's word and the blessed influence of Jesus are excluded, should wander farther and farther away from the guiding lights of the Gospel, sent to direct the feet of all anxious seekers to the safe and happy shelter of the Father's home on high, until they are lost forever. Children are very easily influenced by the examples set by older people. How very necessary it is, then, that father and mother, and, in fact everyone who comes in contact with children, especially deaf-mute children, should strive constantly by their own conduct to set good examples for them to follow.

But I have digressed a little. It was the custom to furnish those pupils who were much in need of some articles of wearing apparel, etc., with what they needed and to charge the bill to parents. If for some reason they could not pay it, the county from which the pupil was sent was required to do so. Knowing this, Carrie Raymond and Julia Keene, on this last afternoon of the term, went up to the matron's room to ask for new hats to wear home. Various needful articles had been distributed to such of the pupils as had made their wants known several days since; Carrie and Julia should have asked then but had neglected doing so. So now, in answer to their requests, the matron said, "I have none to give you, and your old hats will be good enough." And, without giving them time to reply, she shut the door.

Poor girls, what could they do! Carrie knew that if she forced herself into the matron's presence once more and tried to explain how her hat had been sent home to be remodeled and retrimmed, and how she had been vainly expecting it to be sent back to her as her father had said it should be, she would be scolded. And she would rather go without a hat than take a severe scolding along with it. As for Julia, she had torn her old hat up. What were they to do? They would not go home bareheaded; and as the company of pupils with which they were going was to start very early the next morning, some sort of headgear must be secured speedily. Carrie got her old brown calico sunbonnet, mended a rip in it, and decided that it would have to be worn in lieu of anything better; Julia was given an old sun hat.

Before daylight the following morning, a number of the pupils, including Julia and Carrie, were gathered in the library ready to start for the depot. Several persons peered curiously into the brown sunbonnet to see whose head was inside. Carrie took this scrutiny bravely.

As the company were making their way through the dim and, for the most part, deserted streets, Victor Walling came to Carrie's side and asked her if she thought her father wished him to work on his farm again during the summer. "Yes," Carrie replied. So, taking Carrie's bundle, the two walked on together, talking as well as the shadows of approaching day would permit.

A walk of about two miles, almost all the way over paved streets, brought them to the depot. Carrie was glad it was dark, as that fact prevented many from seeing her sunbonnet. The gas jets, twinkling like stars here and there throughout the vast building known as the "Grand Union Depot," looked very pretty, but there was not much time to look about, as the train soon arrived. Carrie, upon entering the cars, concluded that she could dispense with the services of her bonnet for a while. She therefore took it off and placed it out of sight. Her home was only about thirty-nine miles away, and it was yet early morning when her station was reached.

The family had but just finished breakfast when she and Victor Walling reached the home. They were surprised to see them home so early, not expecting them till evening. Rev. Mr. W——, the dearly loved pastor of the family, had intended to take the next train eastward and bring Carrie home in the evening.

19

The Opening of Another Term

Passing over vacation, for the two reasons that it is impossible to keep track of each individual member of the silent throng, and that all vacations are spent in much the same manner as the vacations of children who are not deaf and dumb, we come again to the beginning of another term of school.

There had been some improvements made about the buildings and grounds during the students' absence. The long rows of red desks and stationary chairs in the girls' study room had been removed, and in their place were six long tables, with chairs ranged around them. Racks for newspapers had also been placed along one side of each of the study rooms, and upon these were to be filed various weekly newspapers sent to the institution from different parts of the state. One of the girls' large dormitories had been divided by partitions into small apartments. Some of these apartments would accommodate two persons; others three persons.

From among the girls, a number of the more experienced were chosen to take charge of the small girls who needed to be helped in order to learn to dress neatly, keep clean, and mend and arrange their wardrobes. These older girls, with the small girls placed under their care, were to occupy the new apartments. Similar arrangements had been made for the small boys. Other little changes and improvements had been made, both indoors and out.

The school term was begun under very propitious circumstances. Though many faces that had grown familiar were missed from the silent throng that gathered to resume work, many new faces were seen, some with dreary, apathetic looks that suggested the lack of mental stimulus. On other faces the gleams of intelligence were already visible. In general, there was a marked contrast between those who had been under instruction for some time and those who were but just entering upon their tasks. The former showed signs of refinement, intelligence, and sprightliness of demeanor not, as a rule, seen in the latter.

When the classes were constructed, Carrie found herself in grade number four, with Mr. Vance—the deaf-mute teacher whose skill in imitative pantomime has been already mentioned—as teacher. This arrangement was thoroughly satisfactory to her, for Mr. Vance, in addition to being a first-class teacher, was a man of very pleasant temperament and was much liked by the pupils.

The studies for this grade were scarcely more than a continuation of the studies of the previous term; but there had been one new book added to the list—a reader containing many pleasing and instructive stories. These stories were made very entertaining by Mr. Vance's charming method of making them plain to the minds of his pupils. This he did by acting them out in pantomime, almost as if the scenes they portrayed were actually transpiring at the time. It would no doubt have amused visitors to see him, at times, apparently in deep conversation with some invisible person, or deftly performing household duties with invisible articles.

The lessons explained in the entertaining manner above narrated, were studied by the pupils and then written from memory on the large slates ranged around the wall. The mistakes made in writing them were then noted down in a book kept for the purpose.

This term it was decreed by the superintendent that the advanced classes, one after another, should write short, original compositions, and on certain evenings fixed upon for the purpose, recite them in the presence of the whole school.

Mr. Vance's class was included in this requirement. One day, just before the closing of school for the day, instead of giving a lesson for the evening, Mr. Vance directed his class to employ the evening study hour in writing compositions. The following morning there appeared upon his desk for inspection and correction a large pile of original productions. These showed various degrees of proficiency in the art of expressing thought in the English language. After they had been read, and the mistakes corrected, they were returned to the writers along with sheets of paper on which to copy them. The pupils were then required to study these compositions at odd moments and prepare to recite them.

There were some who considered the task of writing compositions decidedly irksome, but they enjoyed reciting in public. Carrie was not one of this class. She took real pleasure in writing compositions, but shrank from the task of reciting. Her naturally shy disposition rendered her liable to become confused, and she looked forward with dread to the time when she would have to stand up in public and deliver her theme.

A few weeks after the beginning of the term, a gentleman was appointed to teach articulation to such of the pupils who had not altogether lost the power of speech. After tests had been made to ascertain who among the pupils might obtain benefit from instruction in vocal language, several classes were organized. Each class was to receive, each day, an hour's instruction in "lip reading" and other forms of speech. The gentleman entered upon his work with commendable energy; but after a while he apparently began to consider the difficulties in his way too great to be overcome. After some but partially successful efforts to teach "lip reading," or the art of understanding what is said by watching the motion of the lips, he, in the cases of most of those under his instruction, gave up the attempt and confined himself chiefly to hearing and correcting lessons in reading.

Carrie Raymond, who was one of his pupils, was a reasonably correct reader. She had a habit, however, of reading on and on, passing over the periods without stopping to take breath, until her voice became but the faint echo of a sound. To remedy that habit the teacher would sometimes place his hand over the book when a period was reached. At other times Carrie would string the words together in such a manner that they became but a jumble of sounds. Modulation of the voice proved very difficult for these silent ones. So after a while the teacher seemingly grew discouraged. Sometimes he would give Carrie or someone else a lesson to read and then lay his head down upon his desk while the reader proceeded until the end of the lesson was reached. The teacher's head would still remain pillowed upon his desk until his pupils almost fancied him asleep. After a while he would straighten up and resume his duties, but in a rather weary, dispirited manner.

Once, he asked before raising his head from his desk, "Do you see any gray hairs on my head?" Carrie looked sharply among the raven locks, discovered a few silver hairs, and answered accordingly. After these sleepy, and consequently profitless, exercises, Carrie was glad to get back to Mr. Vance's schoolroom and enter into more active duties. Like many another deaf persons, though still in the possession of the power of speech, she had become so accustomed to the use of the silent language of signs that it seemed more natural to her than speech.

Doubtless one of the principal reasons of the failure of all attempts to teach deaf persons to use vocal language fluently arises from the fact that the attempt is not made until they have become accustomed to silent modes of expression. A deaf child in possession of good vocal powers needs, from the very beginning of its education, to have these powers well trained in order to make speech the most natural mode of expression. It has been proved that if this is neglected for any great length of time, and the silent language (which, of course, every deaf person should learn) alone taught, the pupil will be likely to ever afterward choose silent modes of expression.

A hearing and speaking teacher who is engaged in teaching the deaf and dumb, writing in regard to the use of vocal language by deaf persons, says, "It is not natural for persons who are deaf to communicate with those whom they meet, by sounds which they themselves cannot hear; and when this is attempted, the sounds uttered are often so unlike those of ordinary speech as to be difficult to be understood, and disagreeable, and even painful, to the listener."

It is a very common error for deaf-mutes to pronounce words much as they see them spelled, and without the proper accent; when people fail to comprehend their meaning, as is frequently the case, a word or a sentence has to be repeated several times, and, perhaps, then it is not understood. But give an intelligent deaf-mute a pencil and a piece of paper, and he will readily make himself understood.

20

The Magic-Lantern Entertainment

As time went on it was decided that the pupils ought to be enlivened by an entertainment of some sort. Accordingly arrangements were made, and one Saturday evening all the inmates were summoned to the chapel, where they found a great white sheet stretched across the platform.

An instrument somewhat resembling a photographer's camera was placed in front. After all had taken seats, the lights were extinguished and the pupils found themselves involved in darkness. Some who had never witnessed a magic-lantern exhibition were at a loss to know what all this meant. They supposed the lights must have been put out by accident. Presently there appeared in the center of the great white sheet an oval spot of brilliant light while all the rest of the room was still in darkness. By some invisible movement, that little spot of light grew larger and larger until it was about twelve feet in circumference. A moment later there appeared in that oval space a beautiful picture. It was a circle of variegated colors, which, by some hidden movement, was made to revolve, thus presenting a novel as well as beautiful appearance. After that was shown came a representation of our earth, with ships moving over a part of its surface and gradually disappearing from view at one point to reappear again at another. An astronomical scene was represented showing the moon and stars in motion.

Scene followed scene in quick succession. A dog was seen, first barking at a cow, then tossed upward, apparently by the horns of the cow. There was an exhibition of a woman with a very long tongue. A prickly pear was represented, which very unexpectedly opened, disclosing to view a man and a woman with scowling countenances. A rose was also shown, and from amid its scarlet petals emerged a dainty little fairy. A man was seen asleep, and a mouse, stealing from some hidden nook, made its way into his open mouth, a cat springing at it just as it disappeared down his throat. There were pictures of famous edifices and grand natural scenery; also, scenes illustrative of Bible stories. Finally, there appeared the picture of a queer-looking little man. He held in his hand a paper roll. By some mysterious, unseen movement, that was unrolled, and on it was displayed the expression, "Good-night."

The gas jets were again lighted, and the entertainment was at an end. It had been much enjoyed, as was evident from the happy expression on many faces as the pupils filed out of the chapel, and from the fact that it at once became the general theme of conversation.

21

Friendships

The intimate friendship that existed between Carrie Raymond and Julia Keene had not proved very beneficial to either of them. Their natures were such that neither seemed fitted to exert a very strong influence over the other, either for good or evil; but if one of them got into trouble the other was generally a sharer in it, as has been shown in one instance. And here is another.

One day Julia complained of a severe toothache, and Carrie told her that common table salt would alleviate the pain. Julia then asked Carrie to accompany her down to the dining room to get some salt. Carrie consented, but just as they reached the hall leading to the dining room, it occurred to her that a law had recently been made forbidding the pupils from entering the dining room between meals on any pretense whatever. That thought caused her to arrest Julia's progress and remind her of the rule. Julia had forgotten all about it, and now, as it had been recalled by Carrie's words, she stood still, not daring to venture further. As they stood there in the hall, which was perfectly lawful territory, a servant came along and was about to enter the dining room when Julia beckoned to her and requested her to bring some salt. The servant went on into the room and soon returned with a salt dish, from which Julia procured as much as she wanted.

Meanwhile some of the other girls had seen the two going toward the dining room and hurried up to the matron's room to inform her of the fact. The result was that in spite of the assurance of both Julia and Carrie that they had not disobeyed the law, they were severely punished—first, being prohibited from attending for one evening the callisthenic exercises which a lady from the city was teaching the girls; next, when study hour came round, receiving several stinging blows, besides being compelled to stand on the floor for a while. That was about as severe a punishment as any offender usually received, and, in that instance, it was unmerited. While the superintendent and others were inclined to be lenient with the younger and casual offenders, they would not overlook any great offense or allow those who set bad examples to go unpunished.

Once in a while it was found necessary to expel some person who proved incorrigible. But that seldom happened. Most of the pupils entered the school while young, with plastic natures, and could be rightly influenced.

Besides Julia Keene, Carrie Raymond had another friend to whom she was becoming more and more attached. Mary Mayfield was of such gentle, lamb-like disposition that she was a general favorite.

As Carrie's friendship for Mary grew stronger, she was seen less and less in the company of Julia Keene. She was finding in Mary's gentle nature elements that attracted her as nothing in Julia's ever had done. Then, too, Mary was not only gentle, but she was patient, diligent, and conscientious as well. From habitually associating with her, Carrie was, by degrees, acquiring something of her nature. That was evident from the fact that some of her schoolmates began to remark upon her changed manner, and she was much more generally liked than previously.

Mary was thus unconsciously exerting an influence for good over those around her. It may be quite true that

> We shape, ourselves, the "good or ill"
> Of which the coming "years" are made,
> And fill our future's atmosphere
> With sunshine or with shade.

But do we not usually secure our pattern from those with whom we associate? It often seems so.

There was another girl, Addie Jenkins by name, who was a warm friend of Mary Mayfield's, but she very much disliked Carrie. Addie was lithe in form and fragile in appearance, yet she was really much stronger than she appeared; Carrie sometimes received rather rough treatment from her. During that term, however, Addie's rough manner toward Carrie ceased and, like Mary, she too became her friend. Her strength, which had been used against Carrie, was now employed to protect her from any injustice or abuse from others.

One day, some weeks before the Christmas holidays came round, the superintendent entered Mr. Vance's schoolroom and asked him for the names of those of his pupils who were making the greatest progress. Instead of answering his request at once, Mr. Vance replied, suspiciously, "You want to steal them from me!" "Tell me," repeated the superintendent; and Mr. Vance complied by giving the names of Gertie Hawley and Carrie Raymond.

He at once summoned those two girls to follow him, and they proceeded down the long corridor. They felt sure, as they followed him, that they were to be promoted. They were surprised, however, when he passed by the fifth grade and led them on to the end of the corridor and entered the room of the sixth grade! There they were kindly received and shown to seats by the teacher, Mr. Arnold, who was himself a deaf-mute. The superintendent then took one of the girls, who was making but slow progress in her studies, from this grade and placed her in the fourth grade, from which Carrie and Gertie had just been taken. They soon learned that their studies now would be in United States history, intermediate geography, arithmetic, and Scripture lessons. Although Carrie felt gratified at being promoted, she regretted the loss of genial Mr. Vance as a teacher.

Mr. Arnold was an old bachelor and had the reputation of being an austere man. But Carrie and Gertie soon learned from observation that, though he was inclined to be severe toward wrongdoers, he had a decidedly kind heart; as they both endeavored to please him by right conduct, they soon won his favor.

Addie Jenkins was a member of the fifth grade, and every day at recess, or the close of school, she would dart forward and link her arm in Carrie's as the latter passed the door, and then the two would race down the corridor. That soon became so customary that Carrie came to expect it as one of the inevitables. She was therefore surprised when one day Addie failed to make her appearance. Upon inquiring for her, she learned that she was sick, but, much to her relief, she found that she was not dangerously so.

About this time Victor Walling was lying very sick with typhoid fever. A week or so elapsed, and it was announced that he was dead. Some who were with him in his last moments said he had spoken of hearing beautiful music, and Carrie remembered how he had once told her of his desire to hear. He had said that he would willingly give a house full of gold, if he possessed it, to have his hearing restored to him. Though this wish was not granted in this mortal life, he had learned truths from God's holy word to guide him to the "better land," where misfortunes of every kind are unknown. It is believed that in the spirit world, he now lives in full possession of the desired sense of hearing, and, in gratitude, is praising God, saying, "Blessing, and honor, and glory, and power be unto him that sitteth upon the throne, and unto the Lamb forever and ever."

He was a young man of steady, industrious habits, and of good character. He was much liked by his schoolmates. After the funeral services the pupils took a last look at the earthly remains. There was a peaceful expression on the features, as if he had only sunk into a quiet sleep. After the pupils with sober, awestruck faces, on some of which were traces of tears, had filed slowly past the coffin in which he lay, it was taken up and borne away to beautiful Crown Hill Cemetery.

It is a fearful thing to die when the soul is at enmity with God; but when, through repentance and faith in Christ, forgiveness of past errors has been obtained and peace given, the soul can enter "the dark valley of the shadow of death" fearlessly. How needful, then, that everyone should understand the grand plan of salvation as taught in the Bible, and thus be able to come to Christ in full assurance of faith, and obtain through him eternal life.

Victor Walling's death impressed his articulation teacher strongly; so when one of his classes gathered in his room the following day, he, instead of giving them the usual lesson, discoursed upon the uncertainty of life—how unexpectedly death might come to any of us, and the necessity of being prepared for it—after which he dismissed the class. Though at the time his words affected some of them deeply, it is not natural for the heart, in youth, to be long clouded by gloomy reflections or to be permanently impressed by thoughts of death. So, in the rush of events which followed, the sad occurrence was soon out of sight.

22

The Ending of Another Year

On the morning of the day before Christmas, Mr. Arnold directed two of his pupils to go and look in the bookcase. "What for?" asked one. "Oh, go and see," was his response. Wonderingly the command was obeyed, and there were found on one of the shelves a number of small storybooks. Upon opening some of these there was discovered on the flyleaf of each one the name of some member of the class and also a Christmas greeting. One after another being opened, and the names read, they were then conveyed to the persons whose names they contained. All but one of them received a neat little storybook, the remaining pupil, Robert Holmes, receiving, instead, a beautifully bound copy of the Bible. These unexpected Christmas presents from the teacher were appreciated by the recipients.

This term the superintendent had decided to allow all pupils whose parents or friends came for them to spend the holidays at home. He had announced this fact some time previous and charged all to remember that they could not go home on any other conditions. Accordingly many had written home informing parents of these conditions, and today quite a number of them were expecting the arrival of parent or friend who would make it possible for them to enjoy a brief visit at home.

School closed at ten a.m. on this day, and Carrie Raymond, who felt quite confident that her father would come for her, proceeded to her room and arrayed herself in holiday apparel, and then she went down to the basement veranda and watched the various persons arriving. It was not long before she caught sight of her father's well-known form, and, hurrying upstairs, she awaited impatiently the summons to the library. It soon came; and upon reaching the door of that room she found quite a number of visitors seated around the room, most of whom were parents or friends of pupils. Carrie's father was pointed out to her, and after the usual greeting, she hurried away to prepare for the journey homeward.

Christmas was celebrated in the usual pleasant manner at the institution, closing with a social party, which the teachers and others endeavored to make enjoyable. The pupils dearly loved an occasional holiday; but they were prone to grow restless, dissatisfied, and even quarrelsome if allowed to remain idle long. The officers were aware of this from experience. So on the day after Christmas, school was reopened once more.

While lessons were being studied and life was going on as usual at the school, the year, which had so blithely taken up the scepter of authority twelve months before, was silently awaiting the coming of his successor. At the beginning of his reign there had been given him by God a book with pages all fresh and fair. Now these pages were crowded with the records of the various events—countless in their number—which had taken place during the twelve months of his reign. Some of these pages were made beautiful by the records of love, mercy, or self-denial; others were blotted over with wrongs. Some bore marks of tears that had been shed; others told of struggles for the right and their triumph. Even the slightest occurrences had been noted down. And now the book, with all its recorded events, was to be returned to God, to be kept by him till the Day of Judgment. Behind was the past, with its deeds never to be recalled; before was the vast unknown, unexplored future, ready to swallow the poor old year up forever. A few more events were recorded, and then the pen of time dropped from his fingers and he was gone nevermore to return. A new year, with a new book in which to record all the events of the year just begun, stepped in to take his place.

23

Public Exhibitions

The holidays were over, and all the absent ones had returned with light hearts and were ready to take up the daily lessons and strive to climb up the ladder of knowledge.

Mr. Vance's class had, soon after Gertie Hawley and Carrie Raymond had been promoted to the sixth grade, given their public exhibition, at which the members of the class had creditably recited their original compositions.

Carrie and Gertie had each been obliged to write another composition after entering Mr. Arnold's class. Arrangements had been made for this class to recite their productions on a certain evening just before the holidays; but unforeseen events had caused a postponement. Another evening, however, had been fixed upon, and every member of the class was busy preparing to do his or her part. Some of them, however, secretly wished that something would again occur to prevent the exercises from taking place. Others as sincerely hoped that nothing would occur to prevent. The designated evening at length arrived.

At the appointed hour the other classes and the teachers gathered in the chapel. Then Mr. Arnold's pupils made their appearance, mounted the steps of the platform, and seated themselves on the row of chairs placed there for their accommodation. They were all dressed in their best apparel and looked quite as intelligent and attractive as would a class of children who could hear and speak. At first they felt rather uncomfortable, with so many pairs of eyes fixed upon them—

at least some of them did; but there were a few who seemed imperturbable on almost all occasions.

When the superintendent, who also occupied a seat on the platform, arose and prepared to announce the name of the first person who would be expected to recite, the hearts of some began to palpitate very fast. None of them knew whose name stood first on the list, and some of them dreaded the task before them.

They were not long kept in suspense, for Gertie Hawley's name was soon called. She came forward in an easy, graceful manner, bowed to the assembly, and delivered her theme without a pause, or any sign of perturbation.

The exercises were enlivened by several amusing performances. One girl represented the folly of building castles in the air by telling the story of a milkmaid who was trudging along with a pail of milk on her head and laying plans for the disposal of the milk so as to receive the greatest profit to herself. Going steadily on, she became so occupied with her meditations that she forgot the position of the pail, and, not being careful to keep it steady, it suddenly lost its balance and fell, the milk coming down in a shower all over the unfortunate maid. That was the end of her castle building.

One of the boys had written of an incident which illustrates another form of folly—pride. The substance of this incident was as follows: The superintendent one day requested a boy to hitch a horse to the great watertight box into which the refuse from the tables was thrown and haul it away to feed the hogs. He prepared to comply. The horse was brought around and hitched; then, raising his eyes, he saw a teacher standing on the balcony, and he resolved to undertake a feat that should call forth the teacher's wondering admiration. With this object in view, he gathered up the lines and climbed up to the edge of the box. There, skillfully balancing himself, he made a vigorous motion to encourage the horse to start. The horse obeyed the signal, and the next moment the driver was floundering in the slop. He got out again and, in the course of an hour or so, was feeling quite comfortable. A good moral to be drawn from this incident would be, "Never undertake to do anything for the sake of winning admiration or applause."

As before stated, Carrie Raymond dreaded public recitations, but when her name was called on this occasion, she arose determined to do her best. Though she began to tremble a little and a slight tremor disturbed her nerves, she made the customary bow, spelled out her subject, and resolutely entered into the task of reciting her composition. She had written a story concerning two poor children being adopted and brought up by a kind-hearted lady of fortune. Without any blundering she finished her story and sat down, feeling much relieved. She had found the task easier than she had anticipated.

The others that followed also did creditably. At the close, the superintendent gave the class a few silent words of commendation; a silent prayer followed, and the assembly was dismissed.

Other classes were to follow with like exhibitions; in the spring, this class was to give another exhibition of their skill.

24

Spiritual Interests

Dr. Mayhews was anxious to have the pupils led into God's spiritual light, and he labored earnestly, with the teachers as his coworkers, to accomplish this end. One Sabbath, at the close of his discourse, he directed all who truly desired to be Christians to come forward to the front of the platform. Upon this request being made, a small but very intelligent boy arose and came forward. A moment later a tall young man followed his example. Soon a number of other boys and girls came forward and stood silently in front of the platform. To them the doctor addressed some earnest words of counsel, bidding them strive to live rightly and to pray for God's help. He assured them he would also pray for them; then, in obedience to a signal, they returned to their seats, some of them with new and deeper impressions of the importance of religion than they had before known.

Two prayer meetings were organized by the girls—that is, they were formed into two companies, including every girl in the school, for the purpose of holding prayer meetings. They met every day in two of the large dormitories and read a portion of Scripture, after which they all knelt down and each engaged in silent prayer, rising from their knees as soon as they had finished, leaving those who were still kneeling to proceed undisturbed.

Though this was a step in the right direction, none of them as yet seemed to have clear ideas or convictions of the nature and necessity of a spiritual change—a newness of heart—which can only be obtained through faith in Christ. They were simply performing these acts of devotion as a duty which they felt they owed to God, and they were not looking forward to, or expecting, any change in their natures. Most of them were not aware that they needed any change. But God, who reads the desires and intentions of the human heart, knew who among them were honest in their purpose to walk in "the straight and narrow way," and he was so shaping their course as to lead their feet thitherward.

Carrie was one of the number who had manifested a desire to be Christians. Though her desire was sincere, she—as is too often the case—relied upon her own strength of will. This, she found, answered very well when life's pathway was smooth and everything went on harmoniously. But when she met with rough experiences, or anything disturbed the harmony of her atmosphere, she began at once to grow discouraged, and sometimes to think it was "of no use" to try to be good. At such times Mary Mayfield's gentle, cheerful disposition proved helpful as an example, and the earnest discourses delivered in the chapel sometimes inspired her with fresh courage. But still she had not learned this most needful lesson, that human efforts, unaided by divine power, cannot be successful to any great extent. She had not learned to look to God for help and guidance, but, still trusting in self, she was "Baffled, and tossed, and driven about/By the winds of the wilderness of doubt."

But God did not leave her to the mercy of these adverse winds. He only allowed them to be a means of discipline, perchance to fit her for the sterner experiences of life and enable her to sympathize with other storm-tossed souls.

One Sunday morning there came to the institution a traveling evangelist of the deaf and dumb. He held a service in the chapel, and, as he was well versed in the deaf and dumb sign language, he needed no one to interpret his sermon to his silent congregation. At the close of his discourse, he announced that he would hold a service in the city in the afternoon for the benefit of deaf-mutes residing there.

At his request, the superintendent readily consented to allow some of the pupils to attend the service. Accordingly, after dinner a number of the boys and girls, most of them belonging to the three highest classes, set off for the church. The girls were so seldom allowed to go outside of the grounds that they enjoyed highly a privilege of this kind when it was granted them.

When they reached the church they were ushered to seats near the pulpit, where they found the evangelist arrayed in surplice, ready to begin the service. On this occasion he knelt in prayer instead of standing, and the deaf and dumb remained seated instead of rising and standing, as was their custom at their chapel service. But they did not bow their heads; they gazed at the evangelist while he, in silent language, offered up a prayer. Arising from his knees, he proceeded to read a passage of Scripture vocally for the benefit of a number of hearing persons present; then he translated the passage into the deaf-mute language. Then came a short sermon delivered first in vocal language and then in sign language. Another prayer followed, and the service closed.

The pupils returned to the institution, some of them, doubtless, benefited by the service, others with hearts untouched.

After this visit the evangelist proceeded on his way to visit other institutions for the deaf and dumb and minister to other souls.

25

Some Birthday Customs

It had become a custom among the classes to give their respective teachers some kind of a surprise on the anniversary of their birthday. On one such occasion, Professor Gilcrist was very pleasantly surprised to find his armchair nicely cushioned, a pair of gold-bowed spectacles reposing amid a wreath of evergreens on his desk, and his schoolroom nicely decorated with evergreens. The surprise had been devised and executed by his pupils.

Professor Gilcrist was a man thoroughly devoted to the interests of the deaf and dumb, having thus far spent nearly thirty years in their service. By his kind and considerate conduct toward them, and his ready sympathy with them, he had won the confidence and love of very many of these silent ones.

Professor Vance's birthday anniversary was fast approaching, also, and his class held a council to devise some means of giving that amiable gentleman a pleasant surprise. As their pecuniary resources were very limited, the majority not possessing even so much as a penny, they were at a loss how to procure a birthday token. They had generous and loving hearts, and they were greatly desirous of giving their teacher pleasure. After some debating, satisfactory arrangements seemed to have been made, and they at once set about executing them. Mr. Vance's schoolroom was nicely decorated with fragrant boughs and wreaths of evergreens, and a basket constructed of evergreens was hung from the ceiling in the center of the room. In this basket were deposited an orange, an apple, and a cigar.

The following day, when Mr. Vance had somewhat recovered from the fit of abstraction into which this unexpected event threw him and had received the greetings of his pupils and begun his customary duties, the superintendent entered the room. He gazed around for a few minutes, and then his eyes fell upon the pendant basket. While inspecting its contents, he spied the cigar placed there, and immediately his brow knit and a look of displeasure spread over his countenance. Taking the offending cigar from the basket, he crumbled it into fragments; then, stepping to a window, he raised the sash and sent them fluttering to the ground. Closing the window and approaching Mr. Vance, he remarked that smoking was a bad habit, and he did not wish him to indulge in it. Mr. Vance, being a man of good sense and not in the habit of smoking or chewing the weed, cheerfully acquiesced in his judgment. The superintendent had himself been for many years a tobacco chewer, but he had learned the folly of using it and was strenuously exerting himself to overcome the habit. He was also striving to show others the folly of using it, thus to prevent them from going through a course in the hard school of experience.

The little incident above recorded had a salutary effect upon those who witnessed it, judging from the remarks it called forth.

The next day Mr. Vance's wife and his two children, having learned of the surprise he had received, came to inspect the decorations of his room. Mrs. Vance, like her husband, was deaf and dumb, and a stranger would have supposed that their children were also deaf and dumb from the facility with which they used the deaf and dumb sign language. But no! They could both of them hear and speak. The parents, being deprived of the senses of hearing and speech, had habitually used signs as their only means of communicating their thoughts and desires to their children. They had thus taught them the sign language in much the same manner that other children are taught to speak words which they hear others utter. That they understood the meaning of the signs which they used was evident from their intelligently associating them with the objects they represented. Little Helen Vance caught sight of the orange in the evergreen basket, and, pointing up at it, she made the sign for "orange"; then she indicated by the proper signs that she wanted it. So the golden treasure had to be taken from its green cushion to gratify the little maiden.

A few mornings later, a little girl belonging to Mr. Vance's class obtained that gentleman's attention and informed him that it was Alice Ranney's birthday. "Is that true?" he exclaimed, and he seized his ruler and started toward Alice's seat. Alice could not deny the truth of the statement. "How old are you?" he then asked, holding the ruler aloft. Alice refused to tell her age, but someone enlightened him on this point by saying, "fourteen." Thereupon he proceeded to administer fourteen blows, which Alice meekly bore, counting, however, to see that he did not give her a blow too many.

Sometimes an aspiring youth would purchase a handsome birthday present to offer to some girl whose favor he wished to win. Afterwards it sometimes happened that he, fancying himself slighted, would demand his present back. Such a demand was usually complied with.

The deaf and dumb are quite patriotic and disposed to do honor, in their own way, to the great men of our country. All of the pupils in the advanced classes of the I—— Institution knew something of the life and services of the great and good George Washington; so, on the coming anniversary of his birth, some of the boys proposed to celebrate the day in a somewhat original manner. With this object in view they began privately to make their preparations. They petitioned the superintendent to make the day a holiday, and he promised to consider the matter.

On the morning of the 22nd of February the superintendent said nothing about granting a holiday. The morning service passed as usual, and the classes were dismissed to their respective schoolrooms. Then it was that the chief movers in the plan to celebrate the day began to grow anxious, fearing lest their schemes should come to naught. On his way back to his office, after chapel service, the superintendent stepped into one of the schoolrooms for a moment's conversation with the teacher, and, while there, one of the boys ventured to renew the request for a holiday. After some deliberation, the superintendent said he would give them all a half-holiday, to begin immediately after dinner. That arrangement was considered satisfactory by most of them.

As usual, the school exercises were taken up, but it was evident that there was no great interest felt in the lessons this morning. Every now and then someone would venture to make some remark concerning the celebration that was to take place in the afternoon, thus showing whither their thoughts were wandering. I think the teachers must have been very glad when the dinner hour came, relieving them from further attempts to force new ideas into careless, indifferent minds.

The boys hastily ate their dinner and awaited the order to leave the tables somewhat impatiently. When the signal was given, they hurried from the dining room and immediately began preparations to spend their half-holiday pleasantly.

As the day was cold, and a snow lay upon the ground, it was not deemed advisable to allow the girls to go out of doors; so they stationed themselves at the windows to watch the proceedings. The boys who were not to take part in the celebration were kept on their own side of the building so as to afford the girls an unobstructed view; yet as the west windows on both sides faced the grounds where the exercises were to be enacted, everyone had a free view.

It was not long after the girls had gathered at the windows before a number of boys appeared, bearing a small cannon—not a toy, but a real cannon—which they had borrowed from the arsenal in the city. This they wheeled into position and proceeded to open fire upon some invisible enemy. In the opinion of the silent watchers at the windows, it did not make any noise, but simply belched forth a small cloud of smoke.

Presently there was seen skulking among the trees what appeared to be an Indian chief arrayed in Indian war costume. The group around the cannon soon caught sight of him, and several of them went in pursuit of him and soon brought him to where the rest of the group were stationed. They then attempted to converse with him, apparently with only partial success. His queer motions and general appearance were amusing. The cannon was again fired off, causing the poor Indian to jump and quake from fear. After this nothing would induce him to touch the cannon.

Soon there was seen in another direction a young man who seemed endeavoring to escape the notice of the group, but he could not. He was captured and brought forward, and after a speedy examination, during which it was decided that he was the spy (Andre), he was condemned to be hung. Scarcely had the sentence against him been pronounced before his captors proceeded to execute it. Leading him beneath a tree, a bough of which hung conveniently low, they strung him up to the limb, much to the surprise of some of the watchers at the windows. After he had hung for several minutes, he was taken down and carried away while the looks of surprise upon some faces deepened into dismay. It was soon afterwards learned, however, that the *spy* was unharmed. His captors had been so merciful that they had suspended him to the tree by the waist instead of by the neck, and he had leaned his head against the rope so that at a little distance it appeared as if he was suspended by the neck. It was also learned that nothing but powder had been used in the cannon.

The trustees of the institution very unexpectedly arrived during the performance and witnessed a part of it from the library windows. Subsequently, in company with the superintendent, the trustees visited first the girls and then the boys in their respective study rooms.

26

The Sad End of Two Runaways

Notwithstanding the good advice given and the frequent warnings of the consequences of wrong doing, there were a few proud spirits among the pupils who refused to be governed thereby. Of this class were two boys, almost young men, who, growing tired of school life—its requirements and restraints—made up their minds to leave the safe shelter of the institution and wander out into the wide world. Accordingly, one day they secretly left the institution and, boarding a railroad train, started we know not whither. Their funds proved insufficient to defray their traveling expenses, so after they had journeyed some distance, they were compelled to leave the train. They then proceeded on foot, walking on the railroad. When nearing the city of L——, a train approached them from the rear, and, being deaf, they of course neither heard nor heeded the engineer's warning whistle. Before the brakes could be put down and the train stopped, they were both crushed beneath the wheels. When the train was stopped their mangled remains were picked up and borne to L——. Here, the newspaper men were notified of the accident and instructed to report it at once. The coroner was entrusted with the remains, which failed to be identified, and they were buried at the public expense.

The papers of other towns and cities copied the report of the sad occurrence, and it was not long before a copy found its way into the hands of Superintendent Mayhews. He had been greatly perplexed and troubled at the disappearance of the two boys, but as yet he had obtained no clue to their whereabouts. When he read the report he feared that these two disobedient boys were the victims, and he at once started for L—— to view the remains. He returned the following day with saddened countenance and reported to the pupils and teachers, who had gathered in the chapel, the results of his investigation. Said he, "I arrived at L—— and informed the authorities of that town of the disappearance of two of the boys from the institution and of my apprehensions that they were the two who had recently been run over and killed by the cars near that place. After telling my story, I was conducted to the cemetery, and the grave in which the two unfortunates had been together buried was opened. When the first coffin was opened, though the corpse within was badly mangled, I recognized the features as those of Master Ball. The other coffin was then opened, and I recognized Master Scott. So my worst fears were confirmed. There is nothing more that we can do for them now. They have, by their act of disobedience, placed themselves forever beyond the reach of further help. Let this sad, sad occurrence be a warning to you all. Remember what may be the consequence of passing heedlessly by all the good lessons given for your help and safety; and, above all things, beware of taking a step in the wrong direction. Never walk on the railroad track when you can avoid it, and at all times exercise the greatest caution."

The pupils followed the narration of the sad experience of the runaways with feelings of sadness and awe. We trust there were few of them who did not resolve to be very careful not to frequent the smooth, inviting, yet dangerous track of the "iron horse."

27

Some Happenings

One day the articulation teacher, as usual, summoned some of the pupils from different classes to give them an hour's practice in vocal language. The summons was obeyed, but instead of following them into his schoolroom, he stepped into another schoolroom for a few words with the teacher. The pupils awaited his coming for what seemed to them a long while; then they began to grow impatient at his delay and offered a resolution of adjournment. The resolution was carried, and the pupils scattered to their respective schoolrooms. Soon after the teacher returned to find his schoolroom silent and deserted. He proceeded to again summon the pupils who had so unceremoniously and unauthorizedly adjourned. When they had all returned and resumed their seats, he, with a thundercloud look upon his countenance, demanded to know the reason for their strange conduct. "You were not here, and we got tired of waiting for you and thought we might as well go back to our other work," replied one. No further inquiries were made, but the neglected lesson was begun.

When Carrie Raymond and Gertie Hawley, who were members of this grade of the articulation class, returned the second time to Mr. Arnold's schoolroom, that gentleman asked how it happened that they had to take two articulation lessons in a single day. They had to explain how they had deserted on the first occasion.

It was Mr. Arnold's custom, just before the close of school each day, to have the lesson to be studied in the evening written on the large slates where all could read it and he could explain each sentence. The lesson of that day, which was taken from United States history, was duly explained by means of the sign language. Scarcely was that task completed when the teacher on duty for the day flung open the door and announced, "School is closed." Gathering up their books, the girls filed slowly out of the room and tripped gaily down the long corridor, the boys rushing pell-mell in the opposite direction, making a tremendous uproar, of which, however, they were entirely unconscious.

A few moments later Mr. Arnold appeared at the door of the girls' study room and asked, "Where is Carrie Raymond?"

"I do not know," answered the girl addressed, gazing around the room in search of her.

"Where is Carrie Raymond?" she inquired, making the sign by which Carrie Raymond was designated. Some of the other girls immediately took up the sign, repeating it until Carrie, who, seeing them using her sign, inquired what was wanted. "Mr. Arnold wants you," said one of the girls, making that gentleman's sign. It may not be out of place to say here that every person in the institution has a sign which is used instead of his or her name in all cases of personal reference, for the reason that a sign can be more readily understood than the name if spelled out.

When, in obedience to that summons, Carrie approached Mr. Arnold, he said, "There is a box in the library hall for you."

"You may be joking," said Carrie, slyly, half fearing that he was.

"No, I am not," he said. Then he asked, "Is it not the first of April?"

"No," replied Carrie, and she hurried off to get the box. When she reached the main hall, extending between the library and the reception room, she found there a good-sized wooden box addressed to herself. Joyfully picking it up, she carried it off upstairs. As it was the dinner hour, she had to wait until after dinner before she could open it. The box was at last broken open, and she found it to contain a liberal supply of maple sugar, maple syrup, apples, material for aprons, etc. The contents of that box had to be placed under lock and key to prevent them from being taken by those with pilfering tendencies. So every day for several weeks Carrie and a few friends were to enjoy this treat sent by loved ones at home.

That evening, Carrie learned the history lesson given for the following day before the hour for retiring. Instead of sitting idly gazing around the room, she proceeded to learn a few more paragraphs, knowing that thereby she would gain higher credit-marks.

Next morning the pupils in Mr. Arnold's class wrote the lesson from memory without any aid from the teacher and without being allowed to glance over the page of the book to refresh the memory. After the lesson had been written, the pupils changed places and corrected each other's version of it by comparing it with that in the book.

That lesson being over, the arithmetic lesson was then taken up. The pupils were required to work out the examples themselves, after which they conveyed them to the teacher, who corrected any errors that had been made, or illustrated any rule that was not fully understood. Many deaf-mutes acquire a habit of counting on their fingers while solving examples in addition or subtraction. Teachers generally do not approve of that, as they think it hinders mental growth, but many pupils feel at a loss to know how to add or subtract numbers by unaided mental effort. The mental faculties do not seem to work smoothly without the aid of some help from outside; if forbidden to count on their fingers, the pupils, regardless of the rule, will usually continue the habit secretly. Carrie had been in the habit of counting in this way until it seemed more natural to her than any other. She also had a habit of drumming on her desk, or sometimes on the inside of it, with her fingers when counting. Others employed similar means.

To a deaf and dumb person, the fingers are very useful members indeed, serving, as they do, for so many different purposes. But they are often liable to do mischief.

On that day, Mr. Arnold gave permission to those of his pupils who wished to write letters to parents or friends. They accordingly wrote the messages they wished to send, and then placed them on the teacher's desk for correction. While reading the messages Mr. Arnold was surprised to find some complaint about the bill of fare served out to the pupils. One boy had affirmed that there were worms in the gravy placed on the tables. Upon reading that statement, Mr. Arnold arose and expressed his disbelief of it. Thereupon several other boys undertook to corroborate the statement, saying that they themselves had seen little white worms in the gravy.

Mr. Arnold then left the room and proceeded to the kitchen to investigate the matter. Some minutes elapsed, and he returned with a solution of the mystery. The cook thickened the gravy in the usual way, by putting some flour into it; a small quantity of this flour was, during the process, rolled up into tiny masses somewhat resembling worms. The boys, not being familiar with the culinary art, were not aware of that mode of preparing gravy; hence their mistake.

Some of them, doubtless, began to see the folly and injustice of their complaints, especially when they reflected that there was plenty of good, wholesome food served out to them daily, which kept them strong and well.

"Many poor children would deem the institution fare a real luxury," said Mr. Arnold. "Instead of complaining over little trials and hardships, you ought to be very thankful to God, who has afforded you this pleasant shelter and the opportunity to secure an education. Remember that God watches over you with all the tenderness of an indulgent father and regards both your spiritual and bodily interests."

Those uncharitable and complaining letters were revised and abridged, and the writers copied them on sheets of letter paper and prepared them for mailing.

When school closed for the day those little missives were placed in the box intended to receive the mail to be forwarded to persons outside, there to await the coming of the mail carrier.

After supper that evening the girls gathered, as was their wont, in the large, airy, and brilliantly lighted study room, where they awaited with some impatience the distribution of the mail, wondering the while for whom the carrier had brought letters. Presently the teacher who usually conveyed the letters to the girls made his appearance. Almost instantly he was surrounded by a group of eager-looking girls, and four or five hands were simultaneously stretched out to receive the little messages which he held in his hand. After a few tantalizing refusals, he placed the letters in one of the outstretched hands, and the owner of the hand bounded away to a chair, followed by a small swarm of other girls. She mounted the chair, and the other girls crowded around her. The one having the letters proceeded to read the name on the first envelope in the pile. That letter proved to be for Gertie Hawley, and the distributor therefore made the sign by which Gertie was known. Immediately others took up the sign, repeating it eagerly, until Gertie came forward. The name on the next letter was read, and the sign of the girl for whom it was intended was made. That girl happened to be in the crowd, and when her sign was made, she stretched out her hand for the letter. Upon receiving it she danced joyfully away to a cozy nook to read it. The name inscribed on the next envelope was then read, and the letter given to the person to whom it was sent. So one letter after another was distributed, until the pile was exhausted. Many of those who stood in the crowd around the chair had to turn away with empty hands and disappointed looks. The mail carrier, that day, had brought them nothing.

28

The Library—Its Contents— Their Uses and Value

The large and carefully selected collection of books, neatly arranged in rows upon the many shelves of the lofty bookcases in the library room, was a credit to those by whom it was selected. Those who did the selecting had evidently understood the necessity of furnishing the young with pure, elevating, and instructive reading matter. Very few novels had been deemed worthy of a place in the collection. Those that were considered sufficiently wholesome and instructive to be placed there were the works of Charles Dickens, "George Eliot," Nathaniel Hawthorne, Louisa M. Alcott, and Charlotte Bronte. The library also contained Oliver Goldsmith's "Vicar of Wakefield," Miss Mulock's "John Halifax, Gentleman," Miss Phelps' work, "Gates Ajar," and Mark Twain's humorous book entitled, "The Gilded Age." There were also many small books such as are often found in the libraries of Sunday schools. Those contained stories illustrative of the trials and struggles of many of Christ's followers.

In addition to the above, there were books treating of the animal kingdom, books of biography, books descriptive of the ocean and of various lands beyond its deep waters, books containing narratives of thrilling incidents and experiences on land and on sea, fairy tales, books on science, etc.

Some of the books were beautifully bound and some were adorned with bright-colored paintings or gildings, which gave the volumes a very pleasing appearance. Aside from the books, the large and elegant room used for a library contained a cabinet of curiosities such as beautiful shells from the deep sea, corals, etc. There was also a glass case of taxidermied birds. On the top of this case was perched a large, horned owl looking very lifelike, and which evidently could not find room with the other specimens of the feathered tribe inside the case.

Another thing which for a while occupied a place in this room, and attracted much attention, was a model steamboat constructed by a deaf and dumb boy in the institution. It was an imitation of a real steamboat. Its cabin, lower and upper decks, smokestacks, wheel, etc., all looked very natural. On the lower deck were several miniature barrels. The name, neatly painted on one side of this little craft, was "Deaf-mute."

The rules of the institution forbade the pupils to frequent the library, reception room, parlors, the superintendent's office, and the halls between them. They therefore seldom entered any of these apartments unless summoned thither by the officers, or some special errand gave them an excuse for entering.

Although they were not allowed to frequent the library, that fact did not deprive them of the use of the books. Every Saturday evening the librarian selected a number of good books from the collection and carried them either to the boys' study room or to that of the girls. There the older pupils, who knew how to read intelligibly, were allowed to select a volume for perusal. When the selections had been made, the names of the pupils who had taken books were written down in a large blank book kept for the purpose, and the numbers pasted in the books taken were noted down after the names of the persons selecting them. When a book was returned, the number was canceled. By this method the librarian was able to tell in a moment who held any book that was absent from the library.

Though most of those pupils who were privileged to select books to read did so, many of them selected a book with little thought of reading it through; some, seemingly, were chosen only on account of the beautiful binding and the pictures.

A large proportion of deaf-mutes have little or no taste for reading. It is often difficult for them to understand the meaning of what they read, and for that reason they have little interest in the matter. But there are not a few among these who, if they would studiously read all the good books they could find time for, consulting a dictionary at the same time and, when possible, a teacher to enable them to understand what they read, would eventually gain a considerable amount of information which otherwise they are never able to acquire. But it is a lamentable fact that many of them are too indolent or too indifferent to undertake to add to their store of knowledge in that way.

There are others, however, to whom a book or a paper proves a source of real pleasure—a feast enjoyable to the mind—a sumptuous feast. Those who compose this latter class are persons who become deaf only after they have learned enough of reading to enable them to understand simple stories. At first they resort to books as a solace in their misfortune, and then gradually they learn to value them for the thoughts and lessons which they contain.

Carrie Raymond was one of those who could find pleasure and solace in the pages of a book. The first year she attended school at the institution she had begged for books to read; although it was contrary to custom to furnish beginners with books from the library, her request was granted, and she was supplied with reading matter suitable to her age and mental capacity. She had ever since been drawing book after book from the library's generous store and always reading them through. She had thus been enabled to gain many new ideas, as well as to receive much benefit from the noble thoughts contained in some of the books. Others, no doubt, were also benefited.

The value of really good books to the young, and especially to the deaf and dumb, can hardly be estimated; it is to be regretted that a greater number of them are not encouraged to acquire a taste for good reading. They might, by that means, learn to habitually use refined and sensible language in expressing their thoughts. They would also learn much to rightly govern them in their conduct toward others. Then, too, their hearts as well as their thoughts may be elevated and drawn heavenward by invisible force through reading the convincing discourses of thoughtful and observant persons whose lives are consecrated to God.

Much, both of pleasure and profit, is missed by those deaf-mutes who know little of the merits of good reading matter, and yet they seem utterly unconscious of the fact. As before observed, it is often because of their inability to clearly understand what they read. If the books which seem so dull and uninteresting to them are read by some person who fully understands the meaning of what is written, and then translated into the deaf and dumb sign language by that person—that is to say, told in the form of a story by means of the sign language—it becomes quite plain to their understandings and is received with great eagerness. The inability to clearly comprehend the meaning of written language arises not infrequently from lack of encouragement. Sometimes it is from lack of capacity, or the absence of earnest, persistent effort, and is never overcome.

Thus, the deaf-mute is doomed to go through life with but little knowledge of any book except the "book of nature," which he learns by his observations of the actions and conduct of the people with whom he may come in contact. Yet even for such a one, the Bible is not without power. The truths from that holy book, daily taught in the comprehensive language of signs, often sink deep into the heart and are graven upon the mind, becoming a beacon star to guide the unfortunate one safely from earth to heaven. Others exert themselves to a greater degree than those just mentioned and are able to master the sense of what they read. As a result, they are eventually able to understand very much. As a matter of course, they gain a much greater amount of information and exhibit more intelligence than those who read but little.

While reading should be encouraged, one thing should always be borne in mind—that is, the reading should be pure and elevating, else it will do more harm than good. "Satan goes about as a roaring lion seeking whom he may devour"; knowing that he cannot reach the deaf-mute's mind or heart through the sense of hearing, he will endeavor in every other way possible to do so by other means, for he has no compassion for anyone.

The deaf and dumb should be taught that the books and papers which they read may be largely instrumental in shaping their characters, and that a good character is of more value than the most costly gems that sparkle in the crown of a king, and more to be preferred than the wealth of the whole world.

Some deaf-mutes fall into the habit of using slang phrases through reading trashy literature; the minds of others are poisoned; and fortunate are those who escape injury of any kind.

29

Some Little Incidents

One morning, through some mistake, the girls in a certain dormitory were not summoned to the study room when the breakfast bell rang. A few moments after the ringing of the bell—which, of course, they did not hear—some of them came down to the study room, and, finding no one there, they inferred that the other girls must have gone to breakfast. They thereupon hurried down to the dining room and found the door locked. After this unpleasant discovery, some of them proceeded around to a window. Looking in, they beheld their more fortunate schoolmates quietly eating their breakfast.

"Who locked the door?" asked one of them, peering in at the window.

"The matron," answered one of the girls at the table.

The questioner was silent for a moment, knowing if any of the girls inside ventured to unlock the door it would provoke the wrath of the matron, who thought they ought to be punished for their tardiness. "Please give me a piece of bread and butter," she at length said. In response to this request a large slice of bread was buttered, and, the window having been slightly raised, it was slyly passed out to the hungry girl. Several other slices of the good, fresh bread were soon passed out to others.

Meanwhile the remainder of the tardy ones, having also found the door locked, became indignant and proceeded to the superintendent's dining room, which was on the second floor. They informed him of the state of affairs, and he at once, upon learning the facts, left his own meal, proceeded through the teachers' passage down to the pupils' dining room, went straight to the locked door, unlocked it, and threw it open, allowing all who had been shut out to enter. The matron did not interfere; so they all enjoyed their breakfast in peace. However, they wisely resolved to avoid the possibility of a like experience in the future by assembling in the study room more punctually.

The group of large buildings which composed the institution, though spacious enough to accommodate the two hundred or more pupils then occupying them, were, however, not sufficient to afford room for all the deaf-mutes in the state of suitable age and condition to receive an education. The state legislature had therefore appropriated funds to be used in the construction of an additional building. The site chosen for this new building, which was to be of sufficient size to afford all additional accommodations that might be needed for years to come, was between the main building and the school building. Work on the new building had been begun early in the spring. Owing to that work and the time and attention it required from the superintendent, it was decided to close the present term of school in the latter part of May instead of the latter part of June, as was the custom.

Letters were accordingly dispatched to the parents or some friend of each pupil, informing them of the new arrangement. Then preparations for closing school were actively begun. While these preparations were in progress, and the pupils were eagerly counting the days till vacation, two deaf-mute young men from Germany visited the institution. One of them was both deaf and dumb and had been educated by the sign method. The signs which he used corresponded to the signs used by deaf and dumb persons in America, so he found no difficulty in conversing intelligibly with the crowd of deaf-mutes here, who, through curiosity, gathered around him. The other young man was deaf, but not dumb, and, it appears, had been educated by the oral or articulation method and was not familiar with the deaf and dumb sign language. So he was compelled to sit in silence while his companion gave a description of their trip across the ocean and conversed on other topics.

After a while two of the girls observed how lonely he appeared, being unable to join in their silent conversation. As they understood the articulation method, they undertook to converse with him by using it. But they soon found that he had been educated in the German language and did not understand the English language. As they were as ignorant of German as he was of English, they were obliged to abandon the attempt to talk with him.

It was Sunday, so when the hour for afternoon service came, the two young men were invited to attend. They accepted the invitation and were escorted to the chapel. At the close, Dr. Latimer, who had conducted the service, came down from the platform to greet them. He had previously met the one who knew the sign language, but the other was a stranger to him. Upon receiving an introduction to that young man, whom his companion omitted to state was deaf, Dr. Latimer, supposing he was a person who could hear, began talking to him orally. The young man looked embarrassed, and some of the pupils hastened to inform the doctor that he was deaf. "Oh," exclaimed the doctor, apologetically. Then he began talking to him by signs, when his companion said, "He does not understand signs." He now began to feel somewhat disconcerted and soon took leave of the young man. This incident illustrates the advantage of the sign method over the oral method of educating deaf-mutes.

The annual examination of pupils came and passed in the usual manner; and then the pupils, with happy hearts, turned their faces homeward, to enjoy another season of rest and recreation.

30

A Description of the New Building

Work on the new building, which had been begun very early in the spring, was continued steadily during the months of spring, summer, and early autumn, a large force of workmen being employed. By the first of October the greater portion of the building was ready for occupancy.

The superintendent dispatched printed letters to parents or friends of deaf-mute children all over the state, announcing to them that the next term of school would commence on a certain day. He requested that all such children of suitable age and condition to receive an education should be sent to the institution promptly at the beginning of the term. To the parents or friends of those who had already spent some time at the school, he wrote requesting their prompt return.

When the pupils, in response to these letters, returned thus late in the season, they found a large, substantial brick building looming up where once had been a smooth lawn occupied by a pretty greenhouse. The greenhouse had been removed to a flower garden south of the other buildings.

The new building was three lofty stories high. The basement was divided into a large, airy ironing room, a bakery, a kitchen, a storeroom, etc. On the second floor was a spacious and elegant dining hall, which deserves more than a passing notice. The walls and the ceiling—the latter ornamented by massive, carved wooden beams—were tinted a delicate pink. The long rows of lofty windows on each side of the room were shaded by inside shutters.

There were twenty-seven long tables in this room, each of which would afford accommodation for ten persons. Along each side of the tables were rows of yellow chairs. There were five large chests of drawers, with tops like the tables, distributed around the room. Upon those chests, every morning, were to be placed large tin cans, with faucets near the bottom. These cans were intended to hold the hot coffee. Trays on which to convey the cups of coffee from the cans to the tables were placed on the chests ready for use.

In a little room connected with the dining room, on the left, was an elevator which descended into the bakery beneath and was there loaded with bread, or pies, or cakes, and then they were drawn up to the dining room by means of pulleys. The elevator consisted of a number of broad shelves, which, when stationary, formed a sort of cupboard. There was a similar elevator at the opposite end of the dining room, which descended into the kitchen to be loaded with meats, vegetables, etc., which were then drawn up to the dining room. A sort of whistle, placed in the dining room wall, served as the medium to convey a signal to the servants below when more bread, etc., was wanted above.

The tables were spread with white damask tablecloths. A neat water tray, into which to empty the water from the tumblers, was placed at the end of each table. Everything was neat and tidy. The room was, in fact, a model of convenience and comfort.

Besides the dining room, there were on this floor two schoolrooms, a small laboratory, a linen room, the superintendent's office, and, I believe, one sleeping apartment. On each side of the dining room ran a wide hall connecting with both the main building and the school building, so that the pupils would no longer be compelled to go out of doors when going to or from the schoolrooms.

The third floor contained two large dormitories, with bathrooms, etc., attached. Those dormitories, which were spacious and lofty apartments, each contained forty single beds, so white and neatly arranged as to give the rooms a very pleasing appearance. Rows of neat wardrobes extended along two sides of the room. The windows, like those of the dining room, were shaded by inside shutters.

Between the dormitories were the hospitals for those who happened to get sick. Those were very prettily furnished as comfortable apartments and were conveniently arranged for the proper care of the sick. The nurse's room and the medicine room were the only other apartments on that floor, I believe.

The building was surmounted by a cupola, the light from which streamed down into the entry between the nurse's room and the medicine room. All the rooms were furnished with gaslights and were heated by steam conveyed through pipes from a large furnace in back of the school buildings.

Though this new building was far from being as spacious as the main building, it added much to the convenience and comfort of the inmates, besides affording accommodation to many who otherwise could not have been admitted.

31

Persons and Organizations

The number of deaf-mutes who had been admitted to the privilege of the institution this term was greater than ever before, and consequently several new teachers had to be added to the corps of instructors. The articulation teacher, who had at length given up his attempts to teach articulation, or oral language, was appointed to teach one of the regular classes by the sign method. Two deaf persons, who were graduates of the academic department, had also been appointed as teachers. No particular changes were made in the daily routine, but the work was taken up and carried forward in much the same way as it had been during the last term. Those pupils who had passed the annual examination creditably the previous term were advanced one grade.

Under that arrangement, Carrie Raymond found herself in the class only one grade below the academic. Her teacher, Dr. Latimer, was an active, bustling old man with hoary hair and beard. He was genial and kindhearted, but of a rather nervous temperament. In moments of sudden excitement—which were not of infrequent recurrence—he would dash his eyeglasses violently down upon his desk. He more than once broke one of the glasses in that way. On one occasion, when he met with a repetition of the disaster, he grimly remarked that he had to pay fifty cents to have them mended every time he broke them.

Carrie's studies for that term were a continuation of United States history, geography, arithmetic, composition, and Scripture lessons. Dr. Latimer adopted the question and answer system as the means by which to have his class recite their lessons. He wrote the questions where all could see them, and the pupils simultaneously wrote the answers. With crayon and ruler in hand, Dr. Latimer would proceed briskly from one pupil to another, correcting the mistakes made in composing the answers, sometimes adding a pleasant word of encouragement, making some witty remark, or playfully tapping someone with his ruler.

He had been a doctor, by profession, before he began the work of teaching the deaf and dumb, and the sign by which he was known to the inmates of the institution was that made by placing the fingers on the pulse in the manner that a doctor does when examining a patient. The signs by which others in the institution were known cannot be so clearly described in words.

A few weeks after the opening of the term of school, a Sunday school was organized to take the place of the Sunday afternoon lectures. The throng of silent children who were to compose this Sunday school could not, of course, sing beautiful songs of praise to God as other Sunday school children do; still, the idea of having a Sunday school was gratifying to them, and the fact that it must be conducted in silence throughout did not mar their happiness. So every Sunday when the hour for Sunday school came round, they filed into the chapel, where they were soon joined by the superintendent and teachers. When all were seated, the superintendent or one of the gentlemen teachers would advance to the center of the platform, stand in reverent silence gazing upon the assembly for a moment, then slowly extend his hands with the palms open and turned upward. At this signal everyone in the chapel would rise and stand silently gazing at him while he offered up, in signs, a prayer; then bringing the palms of his hands together and moving them slowly downward, the assembly would resume their seats.

At a proper signal one class after another arose and marched out of the chapel, proceeding to their respective schoolrooms, where they were soon joined by their teachers. A few of the classes, with their teachers, remained in the chapel. The Bible lesson studied during the morning study hour was recited. In some of the classes this was done by the teacher asking questions and the pupils answering them; in others, the teacher himself recited the lesson, explaining to the class anything that was not clearly understood. After about three quarters of an hour spent in this way, all once more returned to the chapel, where a limited number of Sunday school papers were distributed. Another prayer followed, and the Sunday school closed.

The exercises were sometimes varied by having some of the pupils learn portions of Scripture, which they would recite the following Sunday.

A debating society had also been organized to meet every two weeks. Its design was to stimulate the mental powers of the pupils and encourage original thought and productions. Mr. Vance was elected president of that society, and Miss Katie Wynn, who had graduated the previous term and was this term elected a teacher, was the "critic." It was, we think, during her connection with the debating society that she wrote the following poem:

I AM DEAF

Bright and beautiful forms of earth
Are moving round and round me;
Playmate, alive with youthful mirth,
Ever loving and kind I've found thee.

The very air in which I move
Seems to be an atmosphere of joy;
All around me are the ones I love;
All seems pleasure, yet 'tis mixed with alloy.

Though I live and move in this fairy scene,
And play an active part with hearty will,
Yet over my hearing there is a screen—
Sweet sounds, to me, are forever still.

The stillness of this gladsome air
Is like a dead calm on the ocean's wave;
Around me all is bright and fair,
Yet sound is hushed—all is silent as the grave.

I list, but cannot hear the sweet birds sing,
Nor hear the breezes that make the forest wave;
I cannot hear the joyous sounds of spring—
All, all is still and silent as the grave.

                                                K. W.

These lines reveal something of the writer's lighthearted, joyous nature. She was not simply a lighthearted, joyous human being, however, for she had a deep love and sympathy for those afflicted like herself and delighted in making them happy. In the plans for the amusement or gratification of the pupils she took an active part, and her pleasant, sunshiny disposition had a genial influence upon many with whom she was brought in contact. Her mission seemed to be to cheer and gladden other lives. And those who were privileged to associate with her were, I am sure, made better by her influence. God's spirit seemed to reign in her heart, purifying and beautifying her life.

One Saturday evening she came tripping into the girls' study room, where she found them all congregated. Some were talking, some dancing, a few mischievous ones were playing little tricks off upon others of their schoolmates, and others were reading. "Do you not want some music?" she asked of the girls near the door. Upon this question being asked, they looked at her in surprise, being, of course, puzzled to know why such a question should be propounded to deaf persons. One of them, however, playfully answered, "Yes, yes." Miss Wynn then tripped away down the hall, passed through the folding doors, and disappeared from view. In a few minutes, however, she again made her appearance, followed by several other teachers and the steward. They ranged themselves all in a row and very gravely began a mock concert by making motions as if playing on different musical instruments. That mimic music delighted the girls more than real music could have done under existing circumstances.

Soon the performance came to a close and the teachers all returned to the library, but only to devise means for further amusements. Presently they returned once more, this time to act out a charade for the girls to solve. After more charades and other like amusements, in which some of the girls took part, they bade them all good night and went back to the library.

Miss Wynn had not always been so cheerful under her misfortune. She related how, when she was a little girl, sometime after she became deaf, she would sit in her little rocking chair and cry and cry because no one would talk to her, not knowing that her deafness proved a bar to the intercourse which she so much longed for. Now, when her own mind had been lifted from the darkness of ignorance into the light of knowledge, and she was enabled to enjoy much that before she could not, she did not forget how lonely and sad she once felt; and she longed to make others, who might feel just as lonely and sad as she once did, happy.

In her endeavors to do that she was also conferring a benefit by keeping little hands, and feet, and eyes, and minds away from mischief's ways. The saying, "An idle mind is the devil's workshop," is just as true in the case of the deaf and dumb as in that of hearing persons, and if they are allowed to grow up in ignorance, how much more applicable it will become!

32

Uncounted Blessings

Thanksgiving Day came round once more, and the silent inmates of our school, could they have had access to the records of the year just past, would have realized that they had very much for which to be thankful to God, the great and beneficent giver of every good and perfect gift, who, in his loving kindness, showers his gifts both upon the grateful and the ungrateful. He had watched over them constantly and tenderly, shielding all from harm save the two boys who, disobeying the rules, left the safe shelter and dared to tread the dangerous track of the "iron horse." He had given them kind and earnest instructors to guide their feet into safe and pleasant paths. He had put it into the hearts of the people to build for them a commodious and comfortable new building and to make a more liberal appropriation of money to supply their daily needs. General good health and happiness had prevailed among them, and today a sumptuous Thanksgiving feast was spread for them in the new dining hall.

After dinner the pupils amused themselves in many ways, and in the evening they had a social party. So ended the day.

"Good morning! Good morning!" said Dr. Latimer, entering his schoolroom in his usual brisk manner on the following morning. Some of his pupils smiled, responsive to his hearty greeting. "Did you have a pleasant Thanksgiving Day?" he inquired. "Yes, yes," was signified by the nodding of heads in different parts of the room. "I am glad," he said; and all at once prepared for the work of the day.

Everything went on smoothly for a while. Presently Dr. Latimer noticed a dissatisfied frown upon the brow of one of his pupils. "What is the matter?" he asked, pleasantly.

"I do not understand my arithmetic lesson," was the reply.

"The machinery of your mind needs oiling to make it run smoothly. Come here," he said.

Carrie Raymond, who happened to be watching him at the moment, laughed softly at his queer solution of the difficulty. The pupil addressed, slate and arithmetic in hand, came forward to have her mind prepared to comprehend the knotty problems. The oiling of the mind's machinery consisted simply in explaining the lesson by means of an example. That seemed to make it work smoothly for a while.

The lesson for the evening was given out, and one pupil after another began to ask the meaning of different words new to them. The difficult words were explained by means of little illustrative stories, pictures, or analogies, or, in some cases, the dictionary furnished a comprehensive explanation.

One day, after their ten minutes' recess, the girls were proceeding rather lazily along the hall toward their schoolrooms when the teacher on duty impatiently exclaimed, "Hurry! Hurry! Life is short!" This assurance was greeted by them with sly merriment, for to them life was very long. In fact, they never stopped to think whether it would really ever end. Many of them but lightly prized the days as they passed, unless they held for them some rare pleasure. But there was one day coming to which all looked forward joyfully. That was Christmas, the crowning holiday of the year.

As Christmas approached, lessons began to be sadly slighted, and conjectures as to what the day would bring seemed to fill every mind.

A number of the girls had secured boughs of evergreens and also had manufactured quite a quantity of white paper roses. The evergreens were wound into festoons, in which the roses were set at intervals. With these festoons they proceeded to decorate their study room, in anticipation of a Christmas party.

Christmas morning came, and some of the girls, with hearts seemingly overflowing with joy and mirth, glided about, spelling with nimble fingers the words *Christmas gift*. The one who succeeded in first saying this considered herself entitled to a gift from the one whom she had taken by surprise.

Knowing something of this sly custom, some of the girls had taken the precaution to tie a bit of scarlet yarn around one finger, which signified, "You are not entitled to a gift from me, for I am armed against all surprises." Nevertheless there were many who had neglected that precaution, and who therefore satisfied their captors by promising them a bonbon in the evening.

The day was spent in much the same way as on previous occasions. There was the usual bountiful dinner. Roast turkey, cranberry sauce, mince pies, etc., were served, and the appetite of everyone was fully satisfied before the order was given to rise from the tables.

After dinner the girls proceeded to get the long tables in their study room out of the way by placing them one upon another in an obscure corner of their sewing room, which was connected with the study room by a highly arched entry, now wreathed with evergreens and looking like a triumphal arch. After the tables had been disposed of, the chairs and benches were arranged in rows near the wall, thus leaving plenty of open space. As evening approached, the study room began to fill with girls, all arrayed in their holiday attire. To pass away the time till supper they waltzed round and round the room, promenaded back and forth, or gathered in little groups to talk. Deaf-mutes are very fond of talking—much more so than of studying. Two girls were observed to be conversing together by watching the motions of each other's lips instead of by using the sign language. An observer would scarcely have believed that they were really quite deaf until convinced of the fact by proper tests. They had learned that method of conversing only by much practice and close observation, both while at home and under the instruction of the articulation teacher at school. That art was a rare accomplishment for deaf-mutes, and so difficult that few attempted to acquire it. The ability to use it, even by those who did acquire it, was often quite limited.

The summons to supper came at last, and all wended their way in orderly file to the dining room. On the tables was found the usual Christmas evening bill of fare—bread, butter, honey, candy, cakes, apples, and tea. When the repast was finished the girls hurried back to their study room, where they seated themselves to await the coming of the boys, who were to be entertained in this room this year. Some of the girls soon grew tired of sitting still, and a few of them, in spite of the fact that they were all told to stay in their seats, would now and then arise and glide across the floor, take a swift glance down the long hall, then hurry back to their seats. After a while one of them, who had ventured on one of these prospecting sallies, announced that the boys were coming, and she hurried quickly to her seat. The other girls suddenly became very quiet, assuming a more decorous attitude than usual—still gazing eagerly toward the door.

A few minutes later, the boys came marching in, some pausing near the threshold to give the girls a general greeting, others passing indifferently up the room. Some crept along, half shyly, and stared curiously around at the decorations of the room, while others glanced along the line of neatly dressed, bright-eyed maidens, evidently in search of some particularly good-looking one for company. Deaf and dumb boys are as fond of pretty girls as are those who can hear, but they are rather shy of the homely ones.

Different games were proposed and entered into with zest. As the amusements that evening corresponded very nearly to those previously described, I will not attempt a detailed account of the party. Enough to say that everyone found some amusement, and there were few who did not feel disinclined to say good night when the small hand of the clock pointed warningly to half past ten. Prayer was offered up to God, and soon the study rooms were dark, silent, and deserted.

33

Pleasures, Tribulations, and Triumphs

The following Friday afternoon, while Carrie Raymond was busy plying the needle in the sewing room, Miss Mayhews entered the room and asked for her. As soon as her name was called, Carrie felt sure that her father, mother, and sister had come for a promised visit to her, but when she reached the reception room she found her father there alone. He greeted her warmly, and then, in answer to a motion from him, she brought him a slate and pencil, and he wrote a few sentences informing her that her mother and sister were in the city visiting her uncle, and that he had come to take her down to see them.

Just then, Dr. Mayhews entered the room, and, after the usual cordial greeting, the two men began conversing. Presently Dr. Mayhews turned to Carrie and said, "You may get ready and accompany your father to your uncle's home."

Carrie bowed an acknowledgment of the permission and was about to leave the room when Dr. Mayhews added, "Your aunt wishes Gertie Hawley to accompany you." Carrie again bowed and hurried off to find Gertie.

Gertie Hawley lived with her grandmother in the city, and during the months of vacation she had attended Sunday school in one of the city churches. Mrs. Wheatland, Carrie's aunt, had been her Sunday school teacher. This is how she came to be acquainted with Mrs. Wheatland and to receive an invitation to visit her.

Carrie soon found Gertie, and, taking her up to the reception room, introduced her to her father, and the two girls hastened away to get ready for their visit.

A pleasant ride of several miles brought them to Mr. Wheatland's neat, substantial residence, where Carrie found not only her aunt waiting to welcome her, but her mother and sister also. The evening passed very pleasantly.

The following morning, Mr. Raymond—who had, during the year, met with some pecuniary losses—told Carrie that he would not be able to get her the usual number of holiday presents this year, and he asked her what she most needed. Carrie, after a few moments' reflection, said, "A popcorn parcher and some black velvet ribbon for my sash." This answer created some amusement among the older members of the group, but Mr. Raymond at once went out and purchased the desired articles.

Mr. and Mrs. Raymond were obliged to take the morning train for home, but Mr. Wheatland insisted on keeping Carrie and Gertie two days longer, although he was aware that for doing so he would owe an apology to the superintendent.

The visit extended over the Sabbath, and the two girls attended Sunday school at one of the city churches. The service was all conducted vocally, and they felt somewhat lonely and out of place on account of their inability to take part in the exercises.

On Monday evening Mr. Wheatland took the girls to the institution in his carriage. As he drove up the avenue inside of the grounds, two deaf and dumb boys passed them, giving the two girls the usual greeting, which was cordially received and acknowledged by a like greeting from one of them and a bow from the other. Mr. Wheatland, who had noticed the greeting and the way it had been received, said, "Why do you allow the boys to throw kisses to you?"

"Oh," explained Gertie Hawley, "they were not throwing kisses, but simply saying 'Good day' in the silent language." Mr. Wheatland seemed inclined to doubt that, but simply smiled.

Upon reaching the institution he asked to see the superintendent, to apologize to him for keeping the girls so long. When he made his appearance he greeted the girls in the same manner as the two boys had done; so Mr. Wheatland was convinced that this was the common mode of greeting. He soon took leave of the girls, who hastened away to tell some of their companions what an enjoyable visit they had.

The following Saturday afternoon Carrie decided to parch some popcorn. So, taking a few ears of popcorn and her new parcher, she went down to the ironing room, where she found some of the servants ironing and a good fire burning. She knew from experience that if she asked permission to parch her corn, she would very likely meet with a refusal, and, being a very self-willed and independent little maid, she went right to work to carry out her plans. One of the servants, seeing her, came up to her and rather harshly told her that she could not parch corn that day. Harsh treatment always aroused Carrie's ire and often rendered her well-nigh intractable; now she stubbornly refused to give up her project. At last the servant seized both corn and parcher and hurled them into the hall, and poor Carrie was obliged to follow them. So vexed was she at that turn of affairs that tears flowed in little streams down her cheeks. Cleo Benton, who had heretofore treated Carrie with cold indifference, noticed her grief and felt touched by it. Inquiring the cause of her trouble, Carrie told her how she had intended to parch some corn and had been rudely sent from the ironing room by the servants. Cleo, in her kindest manner, attempted to comfort her; so potent is true sympathy that she not only succeeded in making Carrie forget the little grievance, but won her gratitude and friendship as well.

It is a singular fact that those who eventually became Carrie's loyal and loving friends had, in nearly every case, almost despised her until some unlooked-for occurrence drew them to her, and they almost unconsciously learned to love her. Carrie was naturally sensitive and reserved, and few were enabled to understand her until brought into close companionship with her. She proved herself a true and pleasant friend to those who treated her justly; but harsh or unjust treatment always aroused her resentment.

Cleo Benton, who had now become one of Carrie's daily companions, one day unwittingly provoked her wrath, and, as a result, a war of reproachful words followed. After that occurrence came a season of gloomy silence, which lasted about an hour. By this time both hearts had lost their wrathful feelings; a reconciliation ensued, and their pleasant companionship was resumed.

The deaf and dumb, as a rule, entertain a very keen sense of their obligation to forgive. At an early period of their education they are taught the Lord's Prayer, in which the Lord himself teaches us to forgive those who injure us if we would ourselves be forgiven. When one of the girls has injured another in any way, she is soon constrained to ask forgiveness. If the offended one still cherishes resentment and refuses to forgive the injury done, the offender will say, "Oh, that is wicked, and God will not forgive you." Then the offended one will say, though sometimes rather coldly, "Yes, I forgive you." At these words the other, throwing her arms around the one she has injured, seals the forgiveness granted by a kiss. Then, and not till then, peace comes back to their hearts and smiles to their faces, as if God, witnessing the scene and knowing they had done the best they knew how to obey his command, manifested his approval by making them happy once more. In the case of the reconciliation of two boys, they, not believing in kissing, clasp each other's hands instead.

One afternoon Carrie Raymond was given a pair of pantaloons to make for one of the boys. Notwithstanding the fact that she had never made a pair before, the work proceeded very well until she had almost finished them. As she was sewing in one of the pockets, she found that the cloth needed to be cut about half an inch to make the work go smoothly together. Instead of taking it to the seamstress to have her fix it, Carrie concluded that she could easily cut it herself.

So she got a pair of scissors—very sharp ones they were—and, not being careful how she used them, before she knew it they had cut their way almost three inches through the cloth, instead of half an inch. Carrie was frightened, and at first she thought of sewing so as to conceal the cut; but she soon found this was impossible. She felt troubled, knowing that the seamstress would be vexed and would perhaps punish her severely. With her sensitive nature, she shrank from harsh treatment of every kind. She sat still, trying to devise some way out of the difficulty, but there seemed no way except to confess what she had done and face the consequences. It was hard for her to do that, and she shrank from it. Still, something told her that was the only right way. So after the sewing hours had ended and the work was all laid away, she went up to her room and, after some hesitation, wrote a note to the seamstress, telling her all about it. It was not, however, until the next morning that she found the courage to knock at her door and give her the note. The seamstress, after she had read it, said, kindly, "I am glad you told me of it. If you had not, I would soon have found it out and punished you. But I will forgive you now, and we will try and remedy the cut." Carrie, with a full heart, thanked her for her kind words, and, with her mind so relieved, hurried away feeling glad she had done as she felt prompted.

34

Winning a Prize

Spring, with its soft, balmy zephyrs, its awakening flowers, its unfolding buds, and its growing grasses, had returned once more. Little birds could be seen flitting gaily from tree to tree, and no doubt were pouring forth a stream of melody, unconscious that their songs were all unheard by the little girls who, with pleased smiles, watched them from the balcony.

It was Saturday afternoon, and the girls, having nothing to do, promenaded up and down the long balcony, strolled about the pleasant grounds of the institution, or watched a number of the officers and teachers who were engaged in playing a game of croquet on the smooth, green lawn. By and by, some of them grew tired of all these pursuits, so they ventured up to the matron's room and asked permission to go down to the greenhouse for a while. This was a thing they were seldom allowed to do, so they felt rather doubtful about being able to secure permission. But upon their promising not to meddle with any of the flowers, and to return soon, permission was granted. Joyfully they hurried to their rooms for their hats, and, arm in arm, strolled down the smooth, macadam drive toward the garden.

They soon reached it and happily found the greenhouse door open. A fountain in the center was throwing a column of water into a cup held in the hand of a statue, from whence it fell to the basin beneath. In this basin were a number of red fish swimming gaily about. Some aquatic plants spread their broad leaves at the water's edge, and a little distance from the fountain grew a lemon tree, upon which were several green lemons. There were plants of many kinds in pots along each side of the greenhouse. After inspecting these the girls passed through a door at the opposite end into a small corridor. Beyond this corridor, through another open door, they caught a glimpse of blooming flowers, whose perfume filled the air. Soon they were making their way along the narrow paths that extended on each side of a pyramid of beautiful hothouse flowers, while above their heads, close to the glass roof, vines, with glossy green leaves amid which gleamed gay-colored flowers, were seen. That lovely scene delighted the girls, and some of them longed to pluck just one flower from the profusion blooming there. But, remembering their promise not to meddle, they refrained.

The superintendent had received a number of nice Bibles of different styles from the American Bible Society. These Bibles, he announced, would be awarded as prizes to those pupils who diligently studied the Scriptures. The first prize was to be given to the one who learned the greatest number of verses by the close of the term. The next, to the one who learned the next greatest number, and so on until the supply of Bibles should be exhausted. Those pupils who concluded to try and win one of the prizes announced their intention to their teacher, who, each Monday morning thereafter, had them write from memory all the verses they had learned during the preceding week. The number learned by each was then recorded in a book kept for the purpose.

Carrie Raymond, who was actively competing for one of the prizes, was taken quite sick before the end of the term, and she had to relinquish her studies and go to the hospital for a while. When that unlooked-for misfortune came upon her, she feared that she might miss winning one of the prizes or else fall far behind others in the race. So she had her Bible brought up to her room, and, whenever she felt able, studied a few verses.

When the last Sunday of the term came—the day fixed for the distribution of the Bibles—all the pupils were summoned to the chapel. There, on a round table, lay the Bibles, ready for distribution. The first name on the prize list proved to be that of a young man of fine personal appearance as well as scholarly attainments. He was called up by the superintendent and requested to make his choice of a Bible. He did so, selecting a large, neatly bound copy, and he then, in a graceful manner, thanked the superintendent for it and returned to his seat. The next name on the list was that of a brother of the first young man. The third name was that of a young lady belonging to the academic class. Carrie was much gratified to find that her own name came next, she having learned the fourth to the greatest number of verses. There were about fifty copies of the Bible for distribution, and none who had kept on studying to win one was disappointed in the expectation of receiving a copy. After they were all distributed the superintendent advised those who had received a copy to study it and try to profit by its teachings.

The examinations had begun the previous week and closed on Tuesday. On Wednesday the graduating exercises took place.

Arrangements for the homegoing were rapidly made. Half-fare tickets were procured for all of the pupils, and certificates entitling them to travel at half-fare on their return trip were also furnished them. Passes were secured for the teachers who were to go with them to see that they reached their homes in safety.

On the day of the departure for home, when Carrie Raymond was seated in one of the spacious railway coaches with a number of her schoolmates and Mr. Vance—who was in charge of their party—the trainboy came along with a basket of prize packages. He paused at Carrie's seat, took up one of his packages, and began talking to her vocally. Carrie could not understand a word of what he was saying, yet she surmised that he was trying to induce her to buy one of his packages. Feeling unable to win a prize that appealed to her purse, she slowly shook her head, thus indicating that she would not take one. But the trainboy, undaunted, still kept up his vocal exercise, and Carrie again shook her head negatively, without effect. Then her companion, a sprightly young lady, made a sign to attract his attention, and, putting her finger to her ear, she shook her head negatively. Then she pointed first to herself and then to Carrie, thus giving him to understand they were both deaf. At this information he picked up his basket, and, rather embarrassedly, moved on.

35

In the Academic Class

Carrie Raymond always looked forward as eagerly as anyone to the vacations at home, and she derived much enjoyment from them. Yet, she was reminded of her misfortune in being deaf when, on social occasions, she found herself almost entirely ignored and compelled to sit in silence, unable to join in the cheery conversation or take part in merry games. Oh, how she longed, at such times, for someone who could sympathize with her and in some way make her forget her misfortune! When she attended church or Sunday school, she wanted to hear the songs that were being sung or the words the minister was speaking, but this, too, was denied her. So she was glad to return to the institution—to companions afflicted like herself, to the silent language which she knew so well, and to the privilege of *seeing* the Gospel preached in a comprehensive form.

She was now in the academic class, with Professor Gilcrist as teacher, whose ripe experience, scholarly attainments, and long service in the interests of the deaf and dumb entitled him to one of the first places in that department of educational work.

In his class, although signs were occasionally used by the teacher in explaining the lessons, they were very seldom used in recitations. The pupils who composed the class had by that time become so familiar with the English language that they could dispense with pantomime. Words spelled by means of the one-hand alphabet and written language constituted the usual means of communication in the schoolroom. But the sign or gesture language, which had become so natural and habitual as a mode of communication, was still used almost wholly in general conversation. In talking in this way, speech can be much abbreviated and still convey the precise meaning intended. In inquiring after another's health one need but make the sign for the word *well* or *sick*, accompanying it with an inquiring look. In speaking of the state of the weather, the signs that express the time and condition need only be used, as in "day cold" for "It is a cold day." In expressing "I am glad," the word *glad* is simply used; and in asking, "Are you glad," the words *you glad*, accompanied by an inquiring look, are used. Such abbreviations, which are numerous, render the sign language very simple and comprehensive. The ease with which thought can be conveyed from mind to mind by means of this language renders it very popular, and it is useless to try to prevent its being employed outside of the schoolroom. But the thoughtful teacher recognizes the necessity of preventing its too free use in the schoolroom, as that would retard the pupil's progress in the correct construction of written sentences.

The academic class was divided into three departments, known as the junior, middle, and senior grades. Those pupils who, upon examination, were judged to be sufficiently intelligent and advanced in the studies of the primary classes to enter this class had, of course, to first enter the junior grade, and, advancing upward, finish the course of study in the senior grade.

The deaf and dumb have neither time, ability, nor inclination to study foreign languages. Nothing but a plain, practical English education is obtainable in the institution. But from time to time young gentlemen graduates of our school availed themselves of the opportunity to obtain a higher education in the college for deaf-mute young men at Washington, DC. The young lady graduates were not privileged to share in these higher advantages.

Some of the girls declared that a change had come over Miss Tyndall, the matron. Many of them had learned to fear, and some to hate her, on account of her austere manner and her apparent lack of sympathy with them. But now she had unexpectedly become quite kind and considerate. They wondered at this change, but nevertheless rejoiced in it. Some of them who had been known to hurry away at her approach in order to be out of her reach, did so no longer. She appeared to be learning to understand that, in order to influence children for good, she must first gain their confidence and goodwill.

Sometime after the opening of the term, a prayer meeting was organized, the one previously organized by the girls having been discontinued. Almost all the pupils of the advanced classes soon became attendants of these meetings, which were held in the chapel every Sunday evening. Some of the teachers also attended, to assist in the services. "If you wish to be followers of Christ you should neither be afraid nor ashamed to confess it," was remarked by one of the teachers when giving the pupils a general invitation to come forward and speak. Thus admonished, some of them, from time to time, would come forward to speak of their desire to do right and be followers of Christ.

There were many, however, who, though they seemed to desire to be Christians, had very imperfect perceptions of what was required of them. They needed much personal help and encouragement in order to enable them to understandingly press forward for the prize of eternal life. Even those who arose to express their desires needed much help and information in order to be able to find their way to Jesus and obtain peace and grace to help in time of need. But little personal help was given, and perhaps it was for lack of this that they remained in spiritual darkness. Too often souls remain needlessly in darkness. God's Spirit knocks at the door of every human heart, not once only, but often, and just as soon as the soul is sincerely desirous of receiving it and manifests that desire by earnestly striving for it, God will find a way to give light.

This fact can be illustrated by the singular conversion of a deaf-mute young lady. It was, I think, during a revival meeting in the town where she lived that she became deeply convicted of sin and earnestly desirous of coming to the knowledge of Jesus as her Savior. But it appears she was perplexed or troubled by some imaginary difficulties. While thus perplexed, she had a vision—whether it was a dream or a waking vision we know not. She thought herself standing on the brink of a deep, wide, dark gulf. She looked across the gulf and saw a person, whom she instinctively felt was Jesus, standing on the other side. He beckoned to her to come to him. She wanted to obey the summons, but the deep, dark gulf between them prevented it. Presently she saw that the gulf was gradually growing narrower. Finally it altogether disappeared, and she found herself at the feet of the glorious personage whom she had seen on the other side. Soon after this she found peace in Jesus.

36

A Pleasant Surprise

"I have concluded that it will be best not to allow any of you to go home to spend the Christmas holidays; but we will try to make a pleasant and enjoyable time for all." Thus spoke the superintendent to the boys and girls gathered in the chapel one morning just before Christmas. Looks of displeasure settled upon more than one fair face at this announcement.

Carrie Raymond, who never could be satisfied with any one thing long at a time, did not at all like this arrangement. She wanted to go home, and she was determined, if possible, to do so. She therefore wrote to her father, saying, "Dr. Mayhews says that he will not let any of us go home to spend Christmas this year, but if you will come for me, I think he can he persuaded to change his mind." Having dispatched this letter, she awaited the result.

"Why do we not have morning prayers in the chapel, as usual?" asked Cleo Benton, in surprise, as the pupils were directed to go to their respective schoolrooms without the usual chapel exercises the day before Christmas. "I presume the heaters are out of order, and the room is too cold for us," replied the person addressed. That theory was accepted as the correct one. But this morning the teachers seemed to have lost all interest in their work, and every now and then would leave their pupils for a few minutes at a time, on one pretext or another, until an idea that something unusual was going on in the chapel began to dawn upon the minds of the more thoughtful and observant among the pupils. As soon as a teacher would leave his schoolroom, and the pupils found themselves

150

alone, down would go books and slate pencils, and arms began to toss wildly about and nimble fingers to convey words of surmise or inquiry, while the play of expression upon the various faces was remarkable. By quick, noiseless signs, or swiftly spelled words, thoughts continued to be conveyed from one to another until the sudden reappearance of the teacher put a stop to it. In one instance, a teacher returning to and entering his schoolroom very unexpectedly found nearly all of his pupils engaged in animated conversation, some of them laughing merrily. Whereupon he quoted, half slyly, half reproachfully, "When the cat is away, the mice will play."

About ten o'clock Carrie was summoned to the library, where she found her father, who had come to take her home to spend the holidays. A few minutes after he came, Dr. Mayhews entered the room, and Mr. Raymond asked permission to take Carrie home; but nothing would induce him to depart from the rule he had laid down. So, at last, Mr. Raymond promised Carrie some nice presents if she would be content to stay, and as Dr. Mayhews gave her permission to go to the city with her father and select the presents, she prepared to do so.

About noon Carrie returned, having just parted with her father at the gates. Going up to her room, she flung down her bundles containing numberless Christmas presents and burst into a torrent of tears. She did not go down to dinner.

After dinner—it being Wednesday, the day on which she had to assist in ironing—one of the girls came to summon her to the ironing room. Now ironing was a task that Carrie very much disliked, and it was not pleasant to think of being obliged to stand almost all the afternoon at a table trying to smooth every wrinkle from dozens of shirts. So she peremptorily refused to go down on the plea that she was tired and did not feel very well. The girl then went away, but Carrie almost feared that someone else would come to summon her—perhaps the woman who had charge of the ironing department. Carrie knew she would speak harshly to her if she should come. Fortunately no one came to disturb her again.

After a while the storm of grief caused by her disappointment in not being allowed to go home subsided, and she began to feel more cheerful. Then she reexamined her presents. There was a nice new shawl, a new dress, and a number of little packages containing candies, nuts, apples, etc. These she placed safely in her trunk and went downstairs and confided the story of her disappointment to Cleo Benton and a few other friends. She said, turning to Cleo, "Will you keep a secret?" "Yes," Cleo answered. So, gathering up the corners of Cleo's apron with one hand, Carrie thrust the other hand into the hiding place thus made for it, and, while Cleo looked into the apron through the small opening left for the purpose, Carrie spelled out her secret. That it was a pleasant secret was evident from the smile with which Cleo received it and the "that is good" which followed the smile.

Carrie seemed determined to believe that Christmas at the institution could not be nearly as pleasant as Christmas at home. In spite of this notion, however, she really enjoyed the day very much.

Some suspicions were entertained that a new program of amusements had been arranged for the day. These suspicions had been awakened by the mysterious movements observed on the previous day. But the hours, one by one, passed, and nothing unusual occurred, till it was thought that these surmisings were unfounded.

Twilight shadows at length spread their mantle over the white-robed earth. The moon, apparently feeling too rich and happy to be selfish, showered its wealth of silvery light upon every object it could reach. But its rays could not penetrate the strong stone walls of the building or light up its inner rooms; so the gas jets were lighted.

Early in the evening all the pupils were ordered to form in line and march to the chapel. Eagerly and expectantly they hastened to obey, chatting and laughing gaily the while. As they filed into the spacious hall, now brilliantly lighted, their bright eyes lit up with surprise and joy as they beheld an immense Christmas tree reaching nearly to the ceiling and loaded from top to bottom with numberless presents. Bright-colored gauze bags filled with bonbons and popcorn formed a background for this tree with its strange fruit; on each side of it was a large basket filled with apples.

In a few minutes the superintendent, who was standing near the tree, put his finger to his ear, assumed a listening attitude, and said, "I think I hear the jingle of bells." A moment later there entered, apparently somewhat hesitatingly, an old man, with long, white hair flowing over his shoulders and a long, white beard reaching nearly to his waist. He was dressed as if prepared to brave the fierce winter blasts, and there were traces of snow on his heavy coat. The assembly gazed at him in mute surprise and amusement. A few among them gave vent to their delight by clapping and waving their hands.

The old man was so well bred that he did not seem to notice this breach of good manners. He bowed, and bowed again. Mounting the platform, he made a speech of jingling rhymes in which he informed the assembly now gazing silently at him that he "had come from the realms of the winter king, over the ice and over the snow, to make them all happy that night." As he made this address in the sign language, the pupils began to suspect that he, like themselves, must be deaf and dumb. When it was finished, he came down from the platform, advanced to the tree, and informed the eager assembly of boys and girls now intently watching his every movement that he was going to give each one of them a present from the tree. With the assistance of the teachers and officers, the presents, procured with money appropriated by the state for the purpose, were distributed.

The names of the few who had accidentally been overlooked were written down, with the promise that they should soon receive a present.

At the close, prayer was offered to the kind Father in heaven, through whom all the blessings enjoyed that day had been received. The apples were distributed as the pupils filed out of the chapel, and a pleasant social party was enjoyed.

When the hour for retiring came, Carrie was compelled to acknowledge that she had enjoyed an unusually pleasant Christmas time.

37

A Departure—Compositions

Just after the close of the Christmas holiday season, Miss Wynne, who had been very sick for several weeks, was taken home. On her departure, she left behind her many sad hearts, for her sunny spirit and helpful ways had endeared her to many beside her own class of little boys and girls. But there was comfort to them in the thought that by and by she would certainly return fully restored to health.

The members of the academic class and those of the two higher primary classes were required, at the end of every three months, to write an original composition. In the writing of these, the pupils were required to rely upon themselves, no correction or help being given them by anyone. The compositions, when written, were carefully arranged in manuscript volumes, which, after being neatly bound in cloth, were placed in the library. The object of this was twofold: First, to ascertain, from time to time, what progress the pupils belonging to these three classes were making in written language, and second, to give any visitors, who might wish to know, a fair understanding of the character of the compositions of educated deaf and dumb persons.

The compositions of many deaf-mutes illustrate forcibly the bent which the moral teachings of the institution give to the mind, and, in many cases, to the heart and life of the individual also. They are a better recommendation of the truths of the Bible than any mere words of praise can be. A composition on "Sunbeams," written by Carrie Raymond, will, in a measure, serve as an example, although different persons have different ways of expressing their thoughts. But few deaf-mutes use figurative terms of speech, being unable, in many cases, to understand anything but plain, literal English.

SUNBEAMS

What are sunbeams? They are minute rays of light which, wandering from their native source, the sun, find their way down to Mother Earth. Here they throw their glimmering light, like a halo of glory, upon the face of great nature, and twinkle and tremble upon the nodding flowers and the running brook. These are nature's sunbeams. But there are sunbeams which, in another sense, are applied to persons who carry light and gladness with them everywhere. These are called the sunbeams of the heart. Little children are often called the sunbeams of the family circle. Their innocent smiles and childish mirth lighten home and make it the one bright spot on earth. Often these little sunbeams early fade and disappear from earth. Then a gloom spreads over the spot once brightened by their presence. It is not strange that it should be thus, for departing sunbeams always leave gloomy shadows behind. But those little sunbeams, though they have taken wings and flown from earth, have not gone out. No, they have winged their flight to a far brighter clime than ours, where eternal sunbeams forever spread their glory around the great Sun of Righteousness, the only true source of perfect light. This divine light bids us all be sunbeams in the journey through life and cover the universe with an ocean of glory. Then let us strive to be sunbeams wherever we may roam. Let us follow the guiding finger of the ever-bright source of light and make him our bright, particular star. Then, though our light may be at first dim and uncertain, let us not suffer dark despair to cast its gloomy shadows around us; but persevere, and it will gradually grow brighter and brighter and cast its luminous glow farther and farther till it disappears from earth, to shine on with untold glory and splendor forever in heaven's eternal realms.

From a composition on "Rooms," written by another deaf-mute, the following is taken.

ROOMS

There are rooms real, fanciful, splendid, plain and homely, bright and joyous, and sad and gloomy. They are various in their character, furnishing, purposes, etc. There are rooms vocal with the melody of dear voices, though these have long been hushed; rooms where people have loved, lived, and died; rooms with histories on walls and furniture; rooms where joy never enters; prison rooms, where the victim broods in silent despair over hopeless fate. The schoolroom, with its bare walls, is very dear to us, for many, many a pleasant hour has been spent therein. There are celestial rooms, which await the coming of the good people in the far-off, beautiful eternity.

Another by Carrie Raymond.

TWILIGHT REVERIES

How many are the thoughts, both sad and joyful, that force themselves upon our minds in the twilight hours! The glorious sun, weary of riding across the azure vault of heaven and pouring his million rays down upon our earth, has bade adieu to the fading day and sunk to rest. From behind the western horizon he throws upward his last bright rays of light, which bathe the western sky in gold and purple; and these brilliant hues, gradually turning to a bright red, melt away into a dull gray, and the darkness of night closing around chases the twilight away. Then it is that, while the last faint glimmers of light come silently stealing through our windows, we call to mind the various events of the bygone day. Some have been sad, and some joyful; and every one of them has been noted by the great Ruler over all and written down in the great book of life, to be accounted for at the last great day. Then it is, too, that we think of our loving and kind Creator, who made all things and gave them all their varied beauty. Then we reflect that, but for him, beautiful twilight, so short and yet so pleasant, could never have existed. And then, again, we think of the twilight of life, which comes in its sad, solemn beauty to mortals, one by one, just before they turn aside from the wearisome journey of life and enter into eternity.

Despite Carrie Raymond's flighty style, her love of using figurative language, her tendency to make her sentences too long, and her occasional grave grammatical errors, she was counted among the best deaf-mute composition writers in the institution. But sometimes she would use figurative expressions, or what she considered brilliant terms of speech, and so freely, too, that common sense was almost, if not quite, left out of sight. But in her mind there were true and reverent, though as yet imperfect, perceptions of truth. Instinctively her thoughts seemed to soar upward and center in God, the only true source of light and truth. But she was not yet a Christian. She had learned much of God's attributes, and of the way of salvation, through the words of her teachers and from much that she had read; but experimentally she knew nothing, or next to nothing, of these. She *knew of* Christ, but she did not *know him* as the Christian does—as a real and ever-present Savior to whom she could go in full assurance of faith and find grace to help in any time of need, to whom she could tell all her troubles, sure of receiving sympathy and strength and help to do right, and bear any cross patiently. No, she had not yet learned to know Christ thus. She was in the habit of praying, it is true, and believed, in a certain sense, that God heard and answered prayer. Yet she had not learned to fully rely upon him for moral strength and courage. She had not learned to see her own utter helplessness and unworthiness or her great need of God's constant help and guidance. She thought she was proceeding onward in the light and needed not to keep seeking light and help. A person asleep in a dark room may dream that she is in a room ablaze with light, and then awake to find that she is still in the dark. So Carrie, though in reality still in spiritual darkness, yet while reflecting upon the glory and brightness of the celestial world and of the joy and peace that reign there, as revealed to her mind by the instruction which she received and the books which she read, fancied that she was in the light. Not until awakened by God's Holy Spirit to a sense of her condition could she realize that she was still in darkness. Not until thus realizing her own weakness and great need she should earnestly plead for the light of life would she receive it.

38

Scenes—Gloomy and Gay

Winter's storms of snow and sleet had ceased and were succeeded by April showers, which bring May flowers, when one day there appeared at the institution a deaf and dumb woman wrinkled and enfeebled by age. She was well known to many of the inmates of the institution, having, in time long past, been a student there, and having of late years made occasional trips thither to sell little trinkets and notions to the girls. She was always warmly received at the institution by the superintendent and his warm-hearted wife, and by many of the other inmates, partly from pity for her in her poverty and loneliness and partly on account of the good traits of character she possessed, which won for her warm friends. She had now, as on other occasions, brought a good supply of trinkets and laces to offer to the girls. These had been supplied from the store of her brother-in-law, to sell for him and also to enable her to make a sort of livelihood for herself. But it was plainly to be inferred from her words and appearance that her life had been clouded by injustice and oppression; she seemed only upheld and kept in the right path by her trust in God and her belief that he could and would, some time, administer justice. The poor old woman seemed to find relief from her troubles by recounting them to the girls who gathered around her. The human heart naturally yearns for sympathy, and these warm-hearted girls, though their own lives were yet unclouded by deep sorrows and trials, nevertheless seemed to comprehend, in a measure, what she had suffered, and their kind and gentle conduct toward her showed that they were sorry for her. She would often speak warmly of the invariable kindness of the superintendent and his wife, Dr. and Mrs. Mayhews, as shown to her.

"Have you brought anything to sell?" was almost the first question asked by the girls who gathered around her on the present occasion. "Yes," she replied. "My basket is up in Miss Tyndall's room, and I will bring it down after supper." So, after the meal, the girls assembled in the study room and eagerly awaited her appearance. It was not long before she came in with her heavy basket on her arm, and soon she was surrounded by a crowd of girls—some of those in the rear climbing upon chairs or upon the table near which she had placed her basket, in order to view the contents of the basket over the heads of their more fortunate companions. From their elevated positions they saw displayed strings of bright-colored beads, cheap earrings and breastpins, laces, ribbons, etc. These things always seem to take the fancy of girls, and those who had money very soon determined to buy some of them. Others, not possessing a cent, could only gaze at the trinkets and laces longingly.

After she had sold a number of articles, the teacher on duty for the evening came in, and the girls had to secure their books, take their places at the long tables, and begin studying the lessons for the following day. So she replaced her things in her basket, and, after watching the girls at their lessons for a while, she retired to rest in the room assigned to her during her stay at the institution.

The following day, before leaving the institution, she enjoyed a pleasant chat with some of the girls. One could see by her conversation that she was intelligent and, if her advantages had been more favorable, she could no doubt have supported herself in comfort. But often the afflicted are turned aside from labor that would enable them to live in comfort, to give place to others untouched by misfortune. We may seek in vain to know the reason for this, just as we seek in vain to solve the problem of why other evils are allowed an existence in the world. But, though we cannot understand why it is so, yet we are assured that God, in his own good time, will right all existing evils and reward every man according to his deeds.

The end of another term was near. The graduating class being small this year, it was decided to have the only member of the middle grade of the academic class assist in the graduating exercises, and also one member of the junior grade. Professor Gilcrist was somewhat at a loss to know who among the pupils in this grade he should choose for the purpose. It was finally decided to determine by vote.

So votes were cast by the members of the middle and senior grades. On the first ballot, Carrie Raymond received the greatest number of votes, although another young lady lacked only one of having as many. A second time votes were cast, and again it was found, upon counting them, that Carrie Raymond had received the greatest number. Carrie was thereupon pronounced the one chosen, and Professor Gilcrist instructed her to prepare an essay for the occasion, which she at once set about doing.

One of Carrie's friends belonging to the graduating class was to recite her essay in oral language instead of by means of signs; Carrie decided that, as she could use this language with enough facility to be understood, she would also employ it instead of signs. As quite a number of visitors who could hear and speak were expected to be present on the occasion, and as the translation from signs into vocal language of half a dozen lengthy essays would be no easy task for him, Professor Gilcrist consented to this arrangement. So every day Carrie might be heard, by those who had ears *that could hear*, loudly declaiming her essay.

Once, while thus employed, the nurse came to the door of the room in which she was seated to ascertain what this vocal exercise meant. Having satisfied herself on this point, she said that it had sounded to her, heard from the hospital, like the voice of a dying person delivering last words. It was not the thoughts of the essay which gave this impression, but the tones of Carrie's voice.

Carrie did not like this opinion of her vocal performance, and she ventured, in company with the other girl who was to recite her essay in the same way, to rehearse before her former articulation teacher. After hearing her recite, he said, "You pronounce most of the words correctly, but you begin a sentence with your voice pitched too high, and it gradually sinks into almost a whisper."

Then he endeavored to show how to rightly modulate the voice, by drawing a series of "o's" of different sizes. These were intended to show how the volume of sound ought to increase or decrease. After one or two failures, he succeeded, in a measure. But her voice had grown weak from long disuse, and it was hard for her to remember how words, the sound of which she could not hear, should be modulated. So she soon forgot the rules explained to her and fell into her old habit.

Early in June, Miss Tyndall, the matron, gave a strawberry and ice cream supper. Strawberries were enjoyed by all nearly every season, but ice cream formed a treat more rare. The supper was an elegant affair. Besides the dishes of strawberries and ice cream, there were candies and cakes. An additional supply of candies that had been procured and placed in the storehouse was overlooked. But a few days later these were placed on the tables, to be equally distributed. A supply of nice oranges was also distributed, each pupil receiving one.

Carrie now felt doubtful of her ability to recite her essay orally without making some blunders. She was therefore much relieved when, on the day preceding graduating day, Professor Gilcrist said that for lack of time both herself and the other lady chosen to assist the graduates would be excused.

Dainty little notes containing formal invitations to attend a party to be given in honor of the graduating class, by Mrs. Mayhews, found their way into the hands of each member of the academic class. The teachers also received invitations.

On the evening appointed for the party the girls of the academic class, all dressed as nicely as their means would admit, assembled in Miss Tyndall's room. Here they were reviewed to see that their toilets were in perfect order. Then tiny bouquets of cut flowers were placed in the hair and on the bosoms of the three graduates, who were, of course, all dressed in snowy white. Carrie and a few others were also in white. When each person had undergone an inspection, they were marshaled into line, and, two by two, they proceeded down to Dr. Mayhews' parlor. Dear, motherly Mrs. Mayhews stood in the doorway and welcomed each one with a kiss as they passed in. They were scarcely seated in the beautifully furnished parlor before the young men of the academic class made their appearance. Mrs. Mayhews, having no kisses to give them, welcomed each one by a cordial handshake, now and then adding a pleasant word as they filed into the parlor.

Presently the young men, one after another, secured a lady for company and marched out of the parlor to promenade the hall or range through other rooms. Carrie was soon approached by one whom she considered decidedly stupid and uninteresting, who asked for her company. At first she was inclined to ask to be excused, but knowing this would be a breach of good manners, she quietly bowed and accompanied him out into the brilliantly lighted hall. He made a beeline for the grand portico. There, planting himself against one of the massive pillars, he stood in silent contemplation. Carrie, who was herself but little given to conversation, waited for him to speak; but he did not do so. Then, thinking that others would consider them both very stupid, standing there doing nothing and saying nothing, she made a few attempts to draw him into conversation. Failing in this, she said, "Please let us go into the library." He assented, and they entered the room. Carrie seated herself on one of the chairs, and he brought another and sat down beside her; but still he remained silent. She again attempted to draw him into conversation without success, as he only answered in monosyllables. At length, in despair, she asked, "Will you excuse me?" He assented by a nod of the head, and she left the library and strolled into the reception room. Here she found more congenial company. But presently a young gentleman attempted to entertain her by informing her how much his new suit of clothes cost. There were others who were much more sensible in their conversation and general deportment, and the evening passed pleasantly.

At ten o'clock supper was announced, and all proceeded to Dr. Mayhews' dining room, where they were served with ice cream, lemon snow, strawberries, cake, confectionery, etc. After partaking of these refreshments, they returned to the parlors, and another hour was spent in strolling about, conversing, or in examining stereoscope views, etc. Then all bade Dr. and Mrs. Mayhews goodnight and retired to rest.

The following day the graduating exercises took place. Among those present to witness these exercises was a representative of one of the leading newspapers published in the city. He took notes of the proceedings, which appeared in the paper the next morning.

Another term, with all its trials and vexations, its tasks and joys, was gone.

39

Events of the Passing Time

Soon after the opening of school in September, the managers of the great Industrial Exposition, then being held in the city, invited all its silent pupils and their teachers to attend the exposition, offering them the privilege free of charge. Of course the invitation was accepted, as anything that added to the happiness or progress of the deaf and dumb was welcomed by Dr. Mayhews.

On the morning of the day designated for the visit, covered express wagons were sent to the institution to convey them to the exposition buildings. Owing to the large number of pupils, it was impossible to secure conveyance for all. So the boys walked and the girls were divided into companies, each company being under the care of a teacher. As fast as conveyances arrived, they were carried to the exposition buildings. That was a grand day to them—a day long to be remembered.

So many things claimed their attention—beautiful things, curious things, and things of utility. Thousands of pictures of different sizes were displayed, from the immense painting representing the "prodigal son"—which occupied a room alone and was valued at seven thousand dollars—to the small cabinet and vignette photographs. There was a beautiful artificial grotto with stuffed specimens of birds and wild animals grouped about on the ledges of rock. An artificial waterfall, pouring over the rocks into a basin beneath, was also seen. Fountains threw their misty spray high into the air. Flowers, fruits, etc., were temptingly displayed. But it is impossible to mention the thousands of beautiful things.

It is sufficient to say that all greatly enjoyed the exposition and returned to the institution with happy and grateful hearts.

The daily experiences of school life passed on as usual. Lessons were studied and learned, household tasks occupied a part of the time each day, and various amusements filled up the leisure hours.

The usual entertainments marked the holidays, and now and then an extra entertainment lent variety to the everyday routine. But these were such as have been already described, and to give details would, I fear, only weary my readers.

Soon after the holidays, cards of invitation were sent to Dr. Mayhews and family, and to a number of the officers and teachers, requesting their presence to witness the marriage of a deaf-mute lady who lived in the city to a deaf-mute gentleman of New York State. The invitations were generally accepted, and on the evening appointed for the ceremony the invited guests gathered at the home of the bride's sister. A minister of the Gospel read orally the questions which composed the marriage ritual, and these questions were translated into signs, as he read them, by one of the teachers from the institution.

After the couple had been pronounced man and wife and had received the congratulations of friends, the question arose as to who had married them—whether it was the minister who had spoken in what was to them a foreign language, or the teacher who had, by means of the sign language, made the questions plain to their minds. It was finally agreed that, by virtue of his office, it was the minister who had performed the ceremony. That question being settled, all proceeded to the dining room where an elegant marriage feast was spread. After partaking of that, a pleasant social time was enjoyed. Wishing the newly married couple a pleasant and prosperous journey together through life, the guests departed.

Time went on, and the genial spring days came once more, when a gloom was cast over the institution by the death of one of its inmates—a little boy who had not been long there and who had seemed, from the first, mentally unable to climb up the "bright rungs" of the "ladder of knowledge." His father was telegraphed for, but being in indigent circumstances, he could not come to view the remains or afford the expense of having the body sent home for burial. So preparations were made to have the body taken to Crown Hill Cemetery, the beautiful city of the dead six miles away, for interment.

It was arranged that about seventy-five of the pupils should accompany the remains, walking a portion of the way and riding in streetcars—which had been specially engaged for the purpose— the remainder of the distance. A funeral discourse was delivered in the chapel; then all filed past the coffin to view the countenance of their little schoolmate for the last time on earth. His face in life had been by no means beautiful, his mouth having been sadly disfigured, as his father had informed the superintendent, by some medicine which a doctor had administered by mistake. But death, or some gracious assurance that had come to him on the approach of death, had stamped his features with a calm, happy look that gave to the poor, disfigured face a comely, pleasant appearance.*

When all had gazed in awe at the still, calm face, the coffin lid was fastened down and it was borne away, followed by a number of the pupils. The funeral concourse moved onward until the beautiful cemetery, with its hills and dales, and its white, glistening monuments and silent vaults, was reached. The sexton was slowly

---

*I do not believe that God will overlook the faults of those, be they deaf and dumb or hearing persons, who, after their minds have been enlightened and they are able to ascertain and obey his commands, still choose to live on in disobedience to what conscience tells them is their duty. But I do not think it is too much to suppose that our kind heavenly Father has provided means of salvation for those who, through circumstances beyond their control, never learn of him, or of his will, in this life. Through the power of Jesus they receive pardon and eternal life, unless, indeed, their souls are so perverted that they are in no way fitted to enjoy this gracious gift.

tolling the great bell that swung from a lofty tower. The whole scene was one to fill the heart with feelings of solemn awe and lead the thoughts to the life beyond the grave.

The pupils marched, two by two, down one of the broad avenues and halted in front of a vault. The body was taken from the hearse and placed therein, after which the graves of three other deaf-mutes were visited. Then all retraced their steps to the streetcars and returned to the institution.

While the daily routine was going on as usual, a little white-winged messenger was borne to the institution, which announced that Katie Wynn had passed through the shadowy valley of death into the unknown life beyond. This intelligence was received with feelings of deep sorrow, for the sunshine of her loving, helpful ways had won for her many warm friends by whom she would be sadly missed. She passed away in the early summertime of life, just when she seemed to be best fitted and most favorably situated to exert a beneficial influence upon others. Why she should thus early be called away, leaving, as it seemed, her work still unfinished, was incomprehensible to her sorrowing friends. They only knew that she was gone, nevermore to return.

At this time a young deaf-mute gentleman was lying ill in the college for deaf-mute young men at Washington, DC. Nearly four years previous he had graduated from the I—— Institution and entered the college for a four-years' course of study. Katie Wynn had been a classmate and warm personal friend of his, and when the news of her death reached him he said, "We will soon meet again." His prediction came true, for death soon called for him. Before he died he spoke of not regretting his hard struggles to gain a good education, although that education was not to prove of the practical value to him that he had hoped it would. Yet it had served as an elevating and refining influence over him during his life, and it is believed that through it, also, he was led to understandingly accept Jesus as his Savior.

40

Harsh Treatment, and Its Results

It was Sabbath morning. The girls, all neatly attired, had taken their places around the long tables in their study room to study their Bible lessons. The teacher on duty for the day, a tall, stately woman whose chief characteristics seemed to be a certain independence and determination of will, had, for the last few minutes, been promenading up and down the middle of the room. She came to the table around which the girls of the academic class were seated and authoritatively addressed Carrie Raymond, saying, "You must not talk." Carrie had just addressed a few words to a schoolmate, as other girls had often done without reproof, but upon being admonished, she at once began studying her lesson. All might have gone well if she had not, as was a habit with her, leaned her cheek upon the palm of her hand and laughed slyly. But this action seemed to irritate the teacher, who returned to her and said, "I must punish you for your sauciness. Go and stand there on the floor."

Carrie protested that she had intended no offense in laughing and that other girls had just been talking as well as herself. "Who are they?" asked the teacher. Carrie gave the names of two of the girls at the table, and they at once acknowledged that they had talked. The teacher quietly passed their offense by, but still insisted that Carrie should go and stand on the floor. Carrie stubbornly refused to obey, feeling that she had done nothing to deserve the punishment. Then, resolved that Carrie should obey her, the teacher decided to use force. Had she known Carrie's nature better and the effect of harsh treatment upon her, it is to be hoped that she would not have attempted force. But, unfortunately, she did not understand her and was only bent upon securing obedience. After vainly attempting to force Carrie to yield, she raised her hand and gave her a stinging blow upon the cheek. This thoroughly incensed Carrie, who at once resolved that nothing should induce her to obey the unjust command.

At length, finding all her attempts futile, the teacher sent one of the girls to summon Dr. Mayhews, but he had not yet returned from church. "Call the matron," the teacher then said; in compliance with this request, the girl went up to the matron's room but soon returned with the information that she, too, was absent. "Summon Mr. Morton," was the next command given. Carrie felt indignant when this command was given, for Mr. Morton was one of the teachers for whom she had a high regard and whose good opinion she greatly valued. If he should come in answer to the summons, he would probably think she had really done something to merit severe punishment since the teacher was so very anxious to have it administered. And, perhaps, he would never think well of her again. But, come what might, she did not intend to yield. She awaited rather anxiously the return of the girl who had gone in search of him, and when she returned alone and reported that she could not find him, Carrie felt much relieved.

All this time, the other girls had been neglected and the study hour had almost passed. The teacher, feeling, perhaps, the uselessness of attempts to force Carrie into obedience, left her for a little while. Presently she left the study room, but soon returned and informed Carrie that the matron was waiting to see her. Carrie thereupon arose from the seat she had so persistently insisted upon remaining in and went into the corridor. There she met Miss Tyndall, the matron, who asked her, not unkindly, why she would not obey the teacher's command. Carrie told her the reasons, adding, "She insulted me."

"No," said the matron. But Carrie insisted that she did so in slapping her cheek, which yet burned.

"Perhaps she did not do the right thing," said the matron, very kindly. "We will not require you to stand on the floor, but I think you ought to ask her pardon for the trouble you have given her."

"I try to do right, but harsh treatment always makes me worse instead of better," said Carrie.

"I am sorry this has happened, but I hope you will try to do right by asking her pardon for the way in which you have acted," said the matron.

She spoke so kindly that Carrie's better nature was won over, and she promised that she would do so. Then she returned to her seat in the study room. The teacher left the study room immediately at the close of the study hour, but Carrie wrote a note to her, asking her pardon for the stubborn way in which she had acted, adding, "If you had tried to govern me by kindness, instead of by severity, you would not have had so much trouble with me." This note she took up to the teacher's room, but, not finding her there, she placed it where it would easily be found and then returned to the study room.

It was not long before the teacher came to her, bringing a note in which she assured her that she was willing to forgive the offense and that she would endeavor to treat her kindly in the future.

Examinations had begun, and the pupils were all confidently expecting to go home the following week, when a very unwelcome guest came to the institution. So rude was this uninvited, unlooked-for guest as to insist on disfiguring the faces of many of the inmates with numberless red blotches. If it had been possible, good, kind-hearted Dr. Mayhews would have unceremoniously turned this guest out of doors in order to defend the pupils from his inquisitive touch, but measles was too powerful for even Dr. Mayhews to grapple successfully. However, Dr. and Mrs. Mayhews and the kind-hearted nurses resolved to nurse the victims until these ugly red blotches had been eradicated. So the large, airy dormitories on each side of the hospital were turned into temporary hospital wards. In these wards the patients were placed and told to lie still and be *patient*. But many of them did not obey this latter injunction to the letter. They wanted to go home, and they manifested their disappointment in not being able to do so at the time anticipated.

Thursday, the 24th of June, came, and those who had before been visited by Mr. Measles and had, therefore, on this occasion, escaped his touch, prepared for the homeward journey. Carrie Raymond, who was among those who had escaped, went up to the girls' ward in company with several others to see their less fortunate schoolmates before leaving. She found about fifty of them lying in the clean, white beds—some of them with faces so disfigured by the red blotches as to be almost unrecognizable.

Soon the institution was deserted by all the pupils save the sick ones. Then, as these, one by one, recovered, they, too, left, to enjoy the bright summer days with loved ones at home.

41

Another Term

The summer vacation passed swiftly, and then Carrie Raymond prepared to return to school. The thought of meeting dear schoolmates and enjoying their companionship was very pleasant to her, but there was another thought still more pleasant—a thought that made her countenance light up with a bright, happy look and brought a tender light into her eyes and a flush of color to her cheeks. What this thought was I leave the reader to guess, and I hasten on with my story.

Some three hundred pupils gathered in the institution at the opening of the term, and yet this number did not comprise one half of the deaf-mute population of the state. Those who were by law granted admittance to enjoy the educational privileges were young. They generally entered at the age of ten or eleven years and finished their seven-year' course of study before they attained the age of twenty. But, this term, there might be seen mingling with the other girls a young woman with a careworn look in her face. She was a deaf-mute who had been kept at home through all the years of her childhood and was then brought there to receive an education. Out of pity for her, as it appeared, the superintendent had departed from established rules and admitted her, although she was twenty-four years of age. Of course she would never be able to acquire more than the merest rudiments of an education. "What a pity that she had not sooner come to receive these benefits!" thought some of the girls, much younger in years and yet far above her in intellectual attainments. Her awkward, dejected appearance contrasted painfully with the quick, intelligent actions and refined demeanor of those who had enjoyed the benefits of the school from an early age. But she was gentle in her manners and showed evidence of possessing intellectual powers which, had they been early trained and developed, would, doubtless, have placed her on an intellectual level with many of her schoolmates. But it was now too late for her to accomplish much.

Carrie Raymond, this term, began the studies of the senior grade of the academic class, having creditably finished those of the junior and middle grades. The senior grade studies were philosophy, chemistry, grammar, rhetoric, and arithmetic. The philosophy and chemistry lessons were illustrated by occasional experiments in the laboratory. During one of these experiments, a glass bottle containing some liquid exploded, ruining the dresses of some of the girls and frightening everyone in the room; but no further damage was done.

The academic class, as before stated, was divided into three grades—or, rather, four, as there were a number of boys preparing to enter the college for deaf-mute young men at Washington, DC. While one grade was reciting, the other grades studied a lesson. The lessons were all recited by the teacher writing one question after another, and the class all simultaneously writing the answers. The teacher gave any needed explanations in the comprehensive sign language. The dictionary, which is generally almost useless to the pupils of the primary classes, proved a source of helpful information to the more enlightened minds of the pupils of the academic class.

This was the year when the women of our land rose up, resolved, if possible, to destroy the power of King Alcohol. All over the land they had formed themselves into bands, and, under the title of the Woman's Christian Temperance Union, were boldly invading the dens where the ruthless king was accustomed to waylay his victims. The news of this invasion, and the cause which led to it, penetrated even to the minds of the silent learners within the walls of our school. The terrible results of strong drink were recounted, inspiring in many of them a wholesome awe of the poisonous drink. This knowledge was, by God's help, to prove a safeguard to many of these silent ones, as it had proved to many of the inmates of the institution before them. The efficacy of these teachings may be proved by the fact that the older boys were allowed to go to the city unattended every Saturday, and none of them save one, whose father was a confirmed beer drinker and lived in the city, were ever known to return drunk. This young man so irritated the superintendent by his habit of drinking beer that he one day informed him, in the presence of his classmates, that he must either refrain from going home on Saturdays or leave the institution. After some reflection, the young man said he would quit going home. "Very well," replied the superintendent. "See that you abide by your decision, for as soon as you break it, the doors will be closed against you."

This term, instead of having but one examination, it was decided to have one every quarter, or every three months. The time for the first quarterly examination came, and the teachers were formed into examining committees. The academic class was to be first examined by a committee of three teachers. Before the pupils had time to compose themselves and arrange for the unpleasant task before them, this committee put in an appearance, and Professor Gilcrist withdrew. Then books were gathered up and laid away, and the work began. The questions were chosen by one of the teachers forming the committee and written on the large slate, and the pupils wrote the answers to the questions as they were presented. The committee then ascertained the number of mistakes made by each pupil, and the examination of this class was at an end. Another committee next examined the highest primary class, and so on, down to the lowest class. The work occupied several days.

I realize that time and space will not permit me to give a detailed account of the events of the term, so I will only attempt a brief outline. The governor of the state, with his officers, visited the institution and expressed themselves as highly pleased with the school. Two of the girls professed faith in Jesus as their Savior and united with the Baptist Church. Death spread his sable mantle over one of the fairest and brightest of the silent band, leaving many hearts to mourn their loss. A dramatic entertainment was given, which corresponded with the Christmas entertainment before described. The girls all enjoyed a visit to beautiful Woodruff Park. Another picnic was held in the woods, and the picnickers, upon their return to the school, found a bountiful feast spread for them under the trees in the park. Other pleasures, trials, vexations, and lessons too numerous to mention filled up the remainder of the time.

Carrie Raymond and others, who had successfully toiled thus far up the ladder of knowledge, were preparing to claim their diplomas. The graduating essays had already been written, and the work of memorizing was going on. Preparations for the party to be given by Dr. and Mrs. Mayhews were being made, the dainty little notes of invitation having already been sent out. But Carrie was in distress. Her cousin, who had volunteered to prepare her graduating costume, had written informing her that it was all complete and had been sent to her address. But the steward had several times visited the express offices in the city in search of it, only to return and report that it was not to be found. All the other girls had received the dainty white dresses that were to form their attire on graduation day, and only Carrie's was wanting. She had almost given up the hope of receiving it and being able to graduate—for she was very particular and did not intend to graduate unless she could do so in style—when it was found and brought to her. "All's well that ends well" is an old adage, and quite applicable in this case.

The party given in honor of the graduates was much enjoyed. The following Monday morning the graduating exercises took place. Carrie, from her elevated position on the stage, saw her father in the assembly and greeted him with a bow, wondering the while how he liked her appearance, but wondering more what a certain other gentleman in the assembly thought of her.

The essays were, as on other like occasions, delivered in signs by the writers and interpreted in oral language by Professor Gilcrist. Then the pupils rose to their feet and stood in silence while Dr. Mayhews awarded the diplomas and, in his usual kind, impressive manner, gave them some parting advice.

Greetings and congratulations soon followed. As Carrie, in company with her father, entered a hack and passed from the institution grounds, she realized that she was leaving a life that, despite its toils and trials, had been very pleasant as well as very beneficial to her. The good lessons she had learned there were not to be left behind, but they were to go with her wherever she went and prove a blessing to her.

42

Conclusion

A certain writer says, "It was customary, as it is now in less enlightened countries, to regard deaf-mutes as imbeciles, and to treat them with neglect. Both from the nature of their affliction and by common consent they were excluded from society."*

Thus regarded, they are doomed to go through life with no knowledge but what they by chance pick up. Think of the isolation, the loneliness, the utter wretchedness of such a life! In this condition the deaf-mute is unable, through his ignorance, to hold communion with other minds by reading books; he is unable, on account of his misfortune, to join in the pleasant conversation of friends or hear the Gospel preached; he knows nothing of God, of his laws, or of salvation through Christ—in fact, thus situated, he is ignorant of almost everything. Surely, such a condition is one to incite pity! Yet the uneducated deaf-mute of the present day is in almost the same condition. But, thank God, there is now a way of escape for him from a life of such ignorance and wretchedness. Yes, experience has amply proved that there is a way of escape; and in this may be seen an additional proof of God's love and care for all his creatures.

Eight years have come and gone since the time of the beginning of my story. The silent children who then for the first time entered upon the pursuit of knowledge in the I—— Institution for the deaf

---

*Editor's note: This quote is from Rev. J. H. Pettingell, "What the Bible Says of the Deaf and Dumb," *American Annals of the Deaf* 26, no.4 (October 1881), 238.

and dumb have grown from boys and girls of ten or twelve years into young men and women, finished their seven- or eight-years' course of study, and left the school. Let us see what changes these years of life in the institution have wrought in them. They came there ignorant, ill-mannered, and in some respects almost helpless human beings. Some of them showed tendencies to vice which needed to be checked. Others had been pampered and humored by overindulgent parents and needed proper discipline to fit them for the sterner experiences of life.

By degrees we have endeavored to trace their progress up the ladder of knowledge. Step by step they have progressed until, instead of being ignorant and helpless, worthy only to be classed with imbeciles, they are in most cases intelligent, refined, and shrewd young ladies and gentlemen. Instead of being burdens to the state and the world in general, they are now enabled to be blessings and helps. Instead of being objects to be looked down upon by their hearing brothers and sisters, they can command their respect and esteem. They have gained a knowledge of God and of his laws; are able to go forth into the wide world, looking unto him for help and strength; and are prepared to fight the battle for the right against the wrong bravely and well.

Soon after Carrie Raymond left the institution, she received a letter from one of the lady teachers, in which she said, "A feeling of sorrow is in my heart because I did not urge you to give your heart to Jesus while you were with me. He has a right to your service. Will you not give it to him?" In reply to this letter, Carrie wrote saying she was by no means indifferent to her soul's interests, and that she was trying to live a Christian life. It is true she was trying to do this, but chiefly in her own strength.

Time went on, and then a series of religious meetings were announced to be held in a little schoolhouse near Mr. Raymond's home. In company with her sister, Carrie one evening attended one of these meetings. After the sermon, the minister invited all who loved the Lord to arise and speak for him. In response to this request several arose and spoke. Carrie's sister arose, as the minister thought, to speak, but in reality to go to a seat in the rear of the room. When he discovered his mistake, he felt prompted to urge those who had not yet realized Jesus to be their Savior to come forward to the mercy seat and seek pardon and peace. He tried to impress upon his hearers the danger of delays.

As the minister proceeded, Carrie observed her sister bury her face in her hands and, finally, arise and hurry to the seat nearest the minister's desk. Then suddenly Carrie herself, for the first time, felt that she was a great sinner under condemnation. A longing to know Jesus as her Savior came into her heart, and she burst into tears. Her mother came to her and asked her if she wanted to go to the seat where her sister was. "What for?" she inquired. "To be prayed for," answered her mother. Yes, she did want to go for that—she felt she needed to. And without a moment's hesitation she went forward and knelt beside her sister. While all were bowed in prayer, she felt more forcibly her need of Jesus as her Savior; she silently prayed, "Jesus, do not pass me by." When she arose from her knees, the minister, who was not acquainted with her, stepped up and spoke to her, seeing which, a friend came forward and informed him that she was a deaf-mute. He looked perplexed for a little while and then ventured to motion to her to arise and speak; but she only shook her head. Then he asked her sister to speak, and she arose, with a face glowing with earnestness, spoke a few sentences, and then, resuming her seat, sat with bowed head.

When the benediction had been pronounced, the two ministers present came to Carrie and shook hands with her, and one of them pointed, joyfully, heavenward. But she shook her head mournfully, for the first time feeling that she was totally unfit to enter heaven. But still she longed to know Jesus as her Savior. She felt that she could never be happy again without the knowledge that he was her Savior indeed. After greeting Carrie, one of the ministers went to her sister and spoke a few words to her, upon which she raised her head and, in a joyous manner, clasped her hands, and, with a face full of earnestness and joy, began speaking. Carrie could not hear a word she said, but she knew, from her happy expression of countenance and her joyous aspect, that Jesus must have received her and spoken peace to her soul. She forgot her own grief and soon felt confident that Jesus would receive her, too.

Two days later she attended another meeting, hoping to go away at its close rejoicing in a Savior's pardoning love. But no encouragement was given her. Everyone—even the minister— seemed to have come to the conclusion that, as she could not hear, the emotion manifested by her at the previous meeting was caused by mere excitement. She went home feeling cast down, but not discouraged, for she felt that Jesus understood her, and that as long as she earnestly sought him, he would care for her.

The next morning she felt constrained to write out a statement of her feelings and convictions to present to the minister. This she did, telling of her unavailing struggles to overcome her temper and self-will. She spoke of having sometimes rebelled against her lot, and thought God unjust in permitting her to be deaf. "But I do not think he is unjust now," she said; and then she spoke of her sincere desire to be a Christian.

The following Sunday morning the minister read this statement to the congregation. That evening another service was held, and Carrie, who had, up to this time, experienced no relief—no change—attended as usual. Just after the first prayer, she felt, as she afterwards expressed it, as if she had been blind all her life and sight had suddenly been bestowed upon her. She realized, as never before, what a wonderful, loving, glorious Savior Jesus is, and her heart exulted in the thought, "He is my Savior." The weary load that she had felt for the last few days was gone, and in its stead were peace and joy. As soon as the service was over she informed the minister and others of the change she had experienced, and they rejoiced with her and gave God the glory.

Life now seemed much brighter, and it possessed a new meaning for her. She began to realize that it was not given for mere selfish gratification. She was eager to press forward and help on the cause of her glorious Master. Little did she know what trials and discouragements she would meet. But she now had the strong arm of an almighty Savior to depend upon for help—a Savior who has said he will never leave nor forsake those who put their trust in him.

Time went on, and the following summer she was baptized. Then a door was opened, as she felt, for her to do service for Jesus. This open door was in the shape of a position as teacher in another institution for the deaf and dumb. We may, at some future time, write of her experience as a teacher.

To Cleo Benton and others, she wrote in glowing terms of the new joy she had experienced; but the replies she received indicated almost indifference on the subject, and sadly she realized that so many do not understand what a precious friend and savior Jesus is. Cleo Benton wrote to her, urging her to quit writing about Jesus and go back to her gay style of letter writing, but she had no taste for that now. And why should she not rejoice that Jesus was her Savior? Why should she not speak of him, since he had done so much for her? She knew that she must still live on surrounded by silence; she knew she must still struggle on in rough paths; but she felt that life would never be the same to her that it once was. Her heart, once so restless and unsatisfied, now found sweet companionship with her new though unseen Friend, and she felt so safe and happy in his keeping. She now understood how Jesus can lighten life's burdens and brighten life's pathway as nothing else can, and she longed to have others understand it, too.

Before closing my story I wish to speak briefly of others of our "silent throng."

Gertie Hawley was for a while engaged to instruct two little deaf-mute girls in private families. Then she married a gentleman who could hear and speak.

Others were also married—most of them to persons who, like themselves, were deaf and dumb—and are living happily. Some—in spite of the tendency to appoint, for the deaf and dumb, teachers who can hear and speak—secured good positions in institutions for the deaf and dumb. Some entered upon other trades for which the training they received had fitted them. One of those who, after finishing the course of study and taking a four-year course of study in the National Deaf-Mute College for Young Men, at Washington, secured a position in government employ that brought him one thousand dollars per annum. A few, who never had much self-respect, became tramps and vagabonds. Some, though well qualified, found themselves unable to secure employment, and so remain quietly at home.

Among those who went out after finishing the course of study, but few were able to testify definitely of the saving power of Jesus. But it is believed that many have since experienced this power and are going on their way rejoicing in a Savior's love, looking forward with gladness to the life beyond the grave and to the time when they "shall see the King of heaven in his beauty," when "the ears of the deaf shall be unstopped, and the tongue of the dumb shall sing."

Let me say just a few more words more concerning Carrie Raymond. The romantic dream of her school days proved to be but a castle in the air, which, by and by, tumbled down; but, strange to say, she did not mourn over its fall. She had begun to rear a structure more enduring, and she went heartily into the work. Of that work in all its completeness only eternity may speak.